P.S. Be EleveN

P.S. Be Eleven

by Rita Williams-Garcia

Amistad
An Imprint of HarperCollins*Publishers*

Amistad is an imprint of HarperCollins Publishers.

P.S. Be Eleven
Copyright © 2013 by Rita Williams-Garcia
All rights reserved. Printed in the United States of America.
No part of this book may be used or reproduced in any manner whatsoever
without written permission except in the case of brief quotations embodied
in critical articles and reviews. For information address HarperCollins
Children's Books, a division of HarperCollins Publishers, 10 East 53rd Street,
New York, NY 10022.
www.harpercollinschildrens.com

ISBN 978-0-06-193862-7 (trade bdg.)
ISBN 978-0-06-193863-4 (lib. bdg.)

Typography by Laura DiSiena
13 14 15 16 17   CG/RRDH   10 9 8 7 6 5 4 3 2 1

First Edition

For Laree, Lisa, Shandese, Kaui, Khari, and Kayla

Contents

A Grand Negro Spectacle

You'd think that after flying six-odd hours from New York to Oakland, then flying six-odd hours back, Vonetta, Fern, and I would be world-class travelers, and those bumps and dips would be nothing.

The 727 still shook, rattled, and rolled from cloud to cloud with no sign of letting up, and we were headed into a storm as we approached New York. The captain said that good old storm was just the thing we needed to cool off the sticky August air waiting to greet us on the ground.

The last thing my sisters and I needed was lightning bolts seeking out plane metal. I kept the fact about lightning's love of big metal objects to myself. No need scaring my sisters with what I knew. They were scared enough.

We had made the best of our flight. For nearly six hours up in the clouds, we couldn't stop talking about meeting our mother, going to the People's Center, and getting to know Sister Mukumbu, Sister Pat, and even Crazy Kelvin. We went on and on about Fern and the Black Panthers at the Free Huey rally. We chanted our mother Cecile's poem—softly, we thought—until the short brunette stewardess came over and cleared her throat. We got the message and stopped softly accusing the world of kidnapping Mother Africa's children.

When we wore out those memories, we went on about the Ankton sisters and their swinging dresses, and about meeting Mean Lady Ming for the first time and being afraid of her. Then we talked about our San Francisco excursion, and eating all those dumplings and fortune cookies. And how the police took our mother away in their black-and-white squad car. But then we'd end up yapping about me riding down that big old hill on Hirohito's go-kart. From there I'd take my fair share of teasing about Hirohito Woods. Then I'd drift off into puffy clouds, thinking a boy liked me, let me ride his go-kart, and promised to be my pen pal.

You'd think we'd save our summer adventures for later, since we'd have to retell them to Pa and Big Ma, but we couldn't stop laughing, remembering, and coming up with plans to get our stories straight. We couldn't tell it all. If we did, we'd never be sent west to see our mother again.

The captain told us to fasten our seat belts. We were coming in for a landing. We held hands and leaned to the left to watch New York come in closer. The bay, roads, buildings, houses, and bushes that were really trees. One hundred butterflies tickled the insides of my belly as the plane went down, down, down. Vonetta and Fern closed their eyes and covered their ears. We all screamed until we met a big bounce against the tarmac followed by smaller bounces and bumps.

Big Ma wouldn't have stood for any screaming coming from her grands, but what Big Ma didn't know wouldn't earn us her shame. Instead, the short brunette stewardess wagged her finger at us. "All of that was uncalled for."

We were supposed to say, "Yes, ma'am," but we didn't.

Instead, Vonetta said, "That landing was scary."

"And bumpity-bump crashy," Fern added.

"It sure enough was," I said.

The stewardess, who was also our airport chaperone, shook her head and told us to stay put until everyone was off the plane. She'd escort us to the baggage claim after she and the other stewardess did the final tidying up.

We unbuckled our belts and waited while mostly men in suits, college students, and a few women with children made their way down the aisle and to the front of the plane. We were anxious to go, but the stewardess chatted on with the captain instead of doing her tidying up.

"We're ready," Vonetta announced to our chaperone.

I shushed her, but the stewardess ignored us, and Fern tugged at my arm and said, "Gotta, gotta," which was her secret code for "I have to make pee-pee." The way she squirmed it wasn't much of a secret.

"Let's go back there." I nodded toward the tail of the airplane, where the bathroom was. I had made her use the airplane toilet while we were halfway through the flight. The flight was too bumpy and she hadn't forgotten it.

Fern shook her head no. She wouldn't go back there again. Not even with the plane parked on the ground.

We got up and marched down the aisle toward the cockpit.

"Excuse me," I said loudly. "We have to get to the bathroom."

"Just hold your horses, young lady. You've held on for this long. You can last a little longer."

Fern's face was turning colors and her eyebrows reached up to say "please, please" so I grabbed Fern's hand, said, "Come on," and we exited the 727 without our chaperone. The three of us went running down the carpeted walkway toward the terminal.

We heard her shouting, "Stop those Negro girls! Stop them!"

Vonetta yelled back, "We're black girls!"

Who cared what kind of "colored" the stewardess called us? I had to get my sister to the bathroom. Fern kept up as best she could while I trotted fast enough to keep my sisters moving forward but not too fast for Fern.

I wished we were back in the days when I could scoop Fern up. We spent one summer with Cecile and all of a sudden Fern was too big for Miss Patty Cake, too big for the night-light, and too big for me to pick her up.

We ran like three fugitives, Vonetta cackling and Fern saying, "Gotta, gotta." Everyone's eyes latched on to us, but I kept my eyes open for restroom signs.

Thankfully we didn't have far to run. Under the restroom sign was a line of women, teenagers, and kids. The line wound outside, but only Fern hopped from one foot to the other or said, "Gotta, gotta," so I pulled Fern past the line and inside the bathroom. Vonetta followed. There was a ruckus, starting with a woman and some kids near the front of the line wearing Mickey Mouse ears. A stall door swung open and I shoved Fern inside while Vonetta and I stood guard. A woman said, "I was next!" Then I said, "We claim this stall for the people." And Vonetta said, "Right on!" and we thought we looked pretty tough standing there guarding the stall for our sister like the Black Panthers guarded the courthouse steps for Huey Newton.

Then this other woman stood before us scolding, "'The people,' my fanny. No one has the right to be rude. You should have asked politely."

A stall door slammed and another woman came out. "Politely? These don't know from polite." She glared at us.

We stood our ground like Panthers standing up to a line of cops.

A lot of good it did Fern. While the women tried to shame us, and Vonetta and I stood our ground, the worst had happened. A clear pee-pee stream ran from Fern's stall down the tiles to the next stall. Fern must not have made it onto the bowl, and the squatter next to Fern let out a stream of words of her own.

Now I was mad at myself for not doing what I should have done: picked Fern up, too big or not, got her in the stall, her shorts down, and sat her on the bowl like I did when she was three.

When Fern came out I checked her shorts. She had at least managed to get them down in time before she sprayed the floor.

There were too many eyes and mouths agape, accusing and murmuring. I led Fern to the sink and turned the knob on.

"Go, Fern. Wash your hands."

Fern's chin stayed pressed to her chest.

"Go 'head, Fern."

Two girls in black Mickey Mouse ears snickered. Vonetta and I cut our eyes at them.

"Where is your mother?" their mother asked. She also wore Mickey Mouse ears. Then all of the women chimed in, and one said our mother should take a firm hand to us.

"Our mother is a soldier in the revolution," Vonetta said.

No one knew what to make of that.

Then the washroom lady pushed her way between the women, the laughing girls, and us.

"Lord, look at that mess," the woman declared. It was just a little stream but she was no one to fool with.

That didn't stop Vonetta. "Lucky thing you have that mop, Miss."

I grabbed Fern's wet hand and Vonetta's, and we made our way around the angry washroom lady and through the line of waiting tsk-tskers and pointers.

My sisters and I ran, dodging through travelers with luggage, and airport workers of all kinds. We followed the signs pointing to the baggage claim area, where we expected to find Pa and Big Ma, and somewhere during all that running we began to laugh.

Sure enough, I saw Big Ma, although I didn't see Pa. Our grandmother's sea-green dress with matching hat and white feather stood out among black, brown, gray, and navy business suits. She was hard to miss.

No one was happier than I was to see Big Ma, who, while I ran with my arms stretched open, didn't seem as tall as she'd always been. But what would we call her besides Big Ma?

We were running and giggling, and just before we were

in hugging range, my long, flapping arms flapped into a newspaper spread open before a gray suit. The paper flew in two directions and I turned and said, "Sorry!" but kept running toward Big Ma, whose arms weren't outstretched like mine. Her hand covered her mouth and her eyes widened like she was watching a horror movie in the dark. Then both hands went from her mouth to her hips.

"Delphine." The "Del" pulled down low and quick and the "phine" had no choice but to follow like a shamed child.

The joy of running and screaming got knocked clean out of me. I stopped running while Vonetta and Fern sped past me and clamped onto Big Ma.

"Yes, Big Ma."

"Delphine. Did you see what you just did?"

My three-second silence went three seconds too long for Big Ma.

"Go over to that white man and apologize for knocking him down. Go on."

"I told him I was sorry," I said.

Her face boiled beneath her hat and wig.

"Del*phine* . . ." Now the "*phine*" spoke her mind. "We're out here in public. . . ." Public meant being out among a throng of white people, and for that I was glad. Their white faces and wide-eyed stares saved me from getting the good side of Big Ma's right hand. All I needed was for the women in the bathroom—led by the

Mickey-Mouse-ears wearers, the washroom lady, and the short brunette stewardess—to come out wagging their fingers and telling all.

The white man in the gray suit, the one whose newspaper I had sent flying, approached us, and I knew I was in trouble. Big Ma both feared white people and placed them up on a pedestal.

The man started out using one of Big Ma's favorite words. "Ma'am," he said, "it was an accident." He was full of smiles, one aimed my way.

"Mister . . ." she told the man, who was older than Uncle Darnell and younger than Pa. "Sir," she started again. "I don't know what gets into children, running in the airport like horses on a racetrack." I doubted the man understood her. Big Ma's "children" sounded like a "churn" making butter, and depending upon how he heard her, her "horses" watered lawns or housed people. His expression didn't stop Big Ma from apologizing on my behalf. "She wasn't brought up to be running in public places. No, sir. She surely wasn't."

The young man was uncomfortable with Big Ma's pleading and apologizing and said again, "It was an accident, ma'am." He folded his newspaper and took off as fast as he could.

If the real Black Panthers and not that fake Crazy Kelvin had seen Big Ma, they would have called her a traitor to her people. They would have drawn an ugly Aunt

Jemima picture of Big Ma with a pig snout and tail, and put it in the Black Panther newspaper, the same way they drew cartoons of the police, and Richard Nixon, who was running for president.

The man's word wasn't enough for Big Ma. She went on scolding, "Delphine. What do you mean running through the airport, knocking down a white man, causing a grand Negro spectacle for all the world to see?"

The more Big Ma carried on, the more she got exactly what she didn't want in the first place. There wasn't an eye that could turn away from us.

Oppression

Big Ma was still talking about the nice white man who didn't have me arrested, whipped, or strung up. She assured me that all of the above would have happened if we were down home in Autauga County, Alabama. For the life of her, she couldn't understand why I didn't humbly and full-out apologize. Didn't I value any of my eleven years and ten months? She said, "It's that no-mothering mother we got to thank for all of this." After paying tribute to Cecile, she swore I had stepped on the known and unknown graves of every Charles, Gaither, and Trotter who had to bow and scrape before the white man to keep from getting strung up in an oak tree or drowned in the Alabama River.

Our suitcases couldn't have arrived any sooner. I

grabbed the largest bag, and Vonetta grabbed the next. Big Ma went to take the smallest bag, but Fern took the handle quickly. "I can carry it," she said, and we lugged our suitcases outside.

The storm over New York had been mild. Barely enough to cool things off.

By now Big Ma had worn herself out scolding me in the names of our family and my lack of good common sense. She wiped her forehead but looked hot and oppressed under her wig and hat. Her "Second Sunday" outfit was soaked around the neck and armholes. There was nothing left to do with her wet handkerchief but to stick it back inside her purse.

We stood at the curb of the terminal where taxis pulled up and wives jumped out of station wagons to kiss their husbands and hand over car keys. A bell captain helped two older girls in jeans and T-shirts get a footlocker and two suitcases inside the back of a Chevy. I made out a blue crown on one T-shirt and under it, COLUMBIA UNIVERSITY. The bell captain slammed the trunk door down, the word NOW in big, bowl-curved letters above the license plate. The back side of the car sagged but everything fit. The bell captain tapped the trunk and the Chevy drove away. My eyes followed the girls and their Chevy, wanting to drive far. Now.

I didn't drift for long. There were people standing a

ways off to the side, also waiting. I didn't have to turn to look at them. The color black atop their heads came through well enough in my side vision. They were the Mickey-Mouse-ears wearers from the bathroom.

I was glad Big Ma had stopped blaming Cecile and me for everything and was now worried about the hot, sticky air and when Pa would drive up "in that car of his."

Only days ago Vonetta, Fern, and I were painting protest signs and shouting, "FREE HUEY!" and "POWER TO THE PEOPLE!" Right now, the last thing I could do was to speak up. The last thing I had was any power at all. The only thing I had from being at the People's Center with Sister Mukumbu and Sister Pat was the word for the opposite of power: *Oppression.* The power to do nothing but keep my mouth shut.

I let Big Ma go on and prayed my sisters wouldn't start talking about the People's Center, the Black Panthers, our adventures in San Francisco, and most of all, Cecile. I just wanted Pa to drive up in the Wildcat and take us back to Herkimer Street.

I heard singing. Two of the kids in mouse ears sang while pointing to Fern, "Pee-pee girl, do a dance. Pee-pee girl. Wet your pants."

Fern cried out, "I did not wet my pants!" She banged her fists against her sides. This would be the point where she'd leap on Vonetta, they'd tussle, and then I'd have to pry them apart.

The kids kept singing their "pee-pee-girl" song, locking their arms in a Mexican hat dance, skipping around to the left, then around to the right. The best I could do was stand to the side of Fern to block her from seeing them and them from seeing her.

Big Ma turned to Fern and said, "Smile at your friends."

Fern folded her arms and said, "They are not my friends."

Then Big Ma was ashamed of Fern, and I was ashamed of Big Ma.

The mother said to the singing and dancing two of her three, "That's enough." All three kids stuck out their tongues at Fern.

Big Ma smiled. She didn't just fear and love white people. She feared and loved their children.

I wanted Cecile to be standing here next to us and not Big Ma. Cecile wouldn't tell us to smile at anyone who tried to oppress us. Cecile would scare them like Black Panthers scare people just by being black and not smiling and by shouting words like *power* and *oppression*.

Finally a Volkswagen bus drove up to the curb and the Mouseketeers waved at its driver. The bus was like one we'd seen in San Francisco painted with daisies, peace signs, and *Flower Power* written in groovy colors. But there were no psychedelic rainbows and groovy words painted on this bus. Just a greenish-blue color with white

14

trim and a white vw below the dashboard. With the bell captain's help, the family loaded up their bus and, one by one, the kids climbed into the backseats. I was glad we'd soon be rid of them. The father got back into the driver's seat, but the mother didn't get in, although the baggage porter was nice enough to open a door for her. She headed straight our way. She walked up to Big Ma and said, "You should have a better handle on these rascals." To me, she said, "You should be ashamed, young lady." She marched over to her Volkswagen bus and climbed into the front passenger seat and the baggage porter slammed the door. Pleased with herself, she clunked down a nod, her Mickey Mouse ears still on.

I turned to face Big Ma to explain. Before I saw it coming, I got the one thing Big Ma always promised in her scolding: the sting of her right hand.

I couldn't stop the tears from rolling down my face. My face burned and the salt trickled down my cheek but I wouldn't utter a sound. The humiliation of being hit like that in front of my sisters hurt more than the slap itself. I held it inside because it was the only power I had.

Big Ma's face was screwed up tight around the lips and jaw but she managed to say, "I don't know what you did, but I know one thing. It was wrong enough for that white woman to come over here, and it was bad enough she thought you had something coming."

Big Ma didn't stop scolding until the bluish-green Volkswagen was well on its way.

Vonetta inched nearer to me and I felt Fern's small hands over mine.

Then I saw the Wildcat.

My GiRl

Big Ma said Pa had been circling around the airport to give her enough time to fetch us. That way he wouldn't have to pay more than the law should allow to sit his car in an airport lot.

The tan-and-black Wildcat crawled up to the curb, its growl low and tame. Vonetta and Fern hopped around as if the concrete below them was too hot to stand on. They flapped their arms crazily and shouted, "Papa! Papa!" before he got the car door open. There was nothing Big Ma could do about it with Pa right there, and I enjoyed that like I enjoyed a Mr. Goodbar all to myself. My feet, however, didn't dare leave the ground, nor did my arms rise up to fly with my sisters'.

All of the windows in Pa's car were cranked down, and Big Ma scolded, "It's your fault they're out of hand," shaking her pointer finger at her oldest son.

My tears had long dried but I wiped my face anyway. Pa swung open the door and stepped out of the car. My heart leapt toward him. No one was as handsome as my father was, even when his face was long, plain, and sad, which was always. Today, he looked chipper, I supposed from being glad to see us after all this time.

Although I didn't jump all over him like Vonetta and Fern did, no one had missed him more than I. In Oakland I saw pieces of Cecile in me, but I knew Pa had his stamp all over me, and I was happy to grow in his shade.

I was first. He leaned down and kissed my cheek twice. If he tasted any salt on my face he didn't say a word. I missed him so much that everything about him seemed new. The freshly cut growth that made the side of his face rough. His cool, shaving-cream smell, with something extra. Not perfume. Men didn't wear perfume. It was woodsier, like standing among Christmas trees. And his shirt was new. Robin's-egg blue. Short-sleeved. Not worn and familiar like all the shirts I'd starched and ironed for him.

Vonetta and Fern were busy jumping and squealing from being tickled by Pa, who usually left the playing around to Uncle Darnell. They didn't notice how new Pa looked.

Big Ma noticed. "Junior! Junior!" She rarely called him that. "Stop all this carrying on in public!" She looked around expecting others to gawk and point at us Negroes, carrying on. Folks cared more about their luggage, taxis, and hugging their own families. That didn't stop Big Ma from being embarrassed.

Pa planted a kiss on Big Ma's cheek like he hadn't driven all the way from Brooklyn with her earlier. She bristled from both not liking it and liking it in spite of pushing him away.

The bell captain blew his whistle for us to get a move on. Pa gave the three of us one more squeeze and loaded our suitcases in the trunk.

"What's the matter, Delphine?"

"Nothing, Papa."

Big Ma chomped at the bit and couldn't be stopped. She was only too happy to report on me. "I'll tell you what the matter is," she began. "You sent them out in that piss-pot of trouble and now she's too big for her britches. As that one goes"—she meant to point at me, but aimed out of the back side-window—"the other two'll follow."

Pa looked in the rearview mirror. My eyes caught his before falling to my lap.

Our lessons on solidarity with Sister Mukumbu at the People's Center hadn't gone for nothing. Vonetta came to my defense. "It's not Delphine's fault she knocked the white man's newspaper down."

Then Fern added, "It's not Delphine's fault I had to *you know* and the line was too long."

Then Vonetta: "And that's why she had to jump Fern ahead."

"Of all those people waiting."

"All those mad people with Mickey Mouse ears."

"And the bathroom lady came."

"Talking about, 'Look at all this mess!'"

"And you told her she had the mop."

"Because you peed on the floor."

Then Fern lurched across my lap and punched Vonetta in the arm. Vonetta socked Fern, and I pulled Vonetta off Fern but Vonetta's fists were still going like spinning bicycle spokes, and Big Ma yelled, "Stop it. Stop it, you wild heathens!" Then to Pa she said, "That's that Cecile in them," like our mother was typhoid. "I tried to tell you." Then back to Vonetta and Fern, "Wait until I get you in the house. Just wait and see what I got for y'all."

And since they had already witnessed how Big Ma hadn't spared me from a small taste of what was waiting for us, Vonetta and Fern pulled apart and settled down on both sides of me.

"And you!" Big Ma's hat and wig turned sideways because she couldn't turn her head all the way around while sitting up front next to Pa. "Wait. Just wait. I'm gonna beat the Oakland out of you. I tell you NOT to go

20

out there in public stirring up a grand Negro spectacle and you make it your business to do exactly that. Don't you know the world's got its eyes on you? But an eyeful isn't enough. No, sir. You haul out the *Amos 'n Andy Show* for all the spectators. Delphine, Vonetta, and Fern, how many times must I tell you, they're always watching. Always."

I prayed Vonetta and Fern knew when a question didn't call for an answer.

"It's that no-mothering mother . . ." Big Ma went on.

"Ma," Pa interrupted, probably to keep her from talking about Cecile. "Your blood pressure."

To that, Big Ma gave a spit sound without actually spitting. "If my pressure don't kill me, these children will."

Pa sighed. "It sounds like Delphine had to get Fernie to the toilet, and Fernie couldn't hold it," he said. He was calm while the Wildcat went back to rumbling.

"Surely couldn't," Fern said.

"That's why you hit everything but the toilet bowl," Vonetta said.

And before they started up, I gave them my own evil eye, and Fern muffled a "she started it."

Big Ma said to Pa, "Junior, there's a right way to go about things and a wrong way. Wrong will get that gal strung up. Mark my words."

"We're in Brooklyn, Ma."

Another spit sound. "Brooklyn. Alabama. You still have

21

to carry yourself just to get by."

Vonetta and Fern hadn't stopped poking at each other. Vonetta said, "I didn't start it but I'm ending it," and stuck out her tongue. Fern couldn't get back at the Mouseketeers who had stuck their tongues out at her, but only one person separated her from Vonetta. Fern tried to kick Vonetta but ended up kicking me, and then Pa said, hard, firm, but not loud, "All right, girls," and put an end to it all. My knee throbbed.

Traffic on the Belt Parkway kept us in Queens longer than Pa had planned. The drive to Brooklyn seemed to go better if no one spoke. We all took the hint, including Big Ma, but we were all thinking about something.

A white woman had spoken to Big Ma about me. I resigned myself to seeing lightning in the whipping of a lifetime. A whipping that would outdo my last whipping at age nine for letting Vonetta and Fern get into the grape jelly. They dropped and broke the glass jar and had grape jelly and glass everywhere, when I should have been watching them.

At least the short brunette stewardess didn't show up to report how we ran away from her.

The Wildcat crouched, leapt, then sat along the Belt Parkway in spurts. Silence had given way to yawning, and then Big Ma, Vonetta, and Fern napped. They slept hard and didn't stir when the quiet got broken up by the Temptations. Not the singers in matching suits, spinning and snapping fingers into one loud pop from the radio. Just one of the Temptations' tunes whistling clear-water cool through Pa's lips. I heard all the words and instruments, complete with stereo highs and bass lows to "My Girl," fluting out of his long but happy face.

HeRkimeR StReet

I felt like a thief trying to steal a good look at my father's face through the rearview mirror. He caught me and winked. For a second it was like having Uncle Darnell with me. Uncle D. Always happy, singing, and still doing the Watusi when that dance had been long gone.

I shuddered as a picture flashed before me. Would my father pick up dancing? The last thing I wanted was a father who danced and carried on like he was fresh out of high school.

As soon as that shudder passed, another overtook it. The gymnasium in June. The sixth-grade dance. The happening no sixth grader could avoid, unless her parents forbade her to go. That wasn't likely. All the PTA mothers

24

looked forward to sewing dresses, teaching their sons to do the box step, and giving assemblies on how sixth graders are expected to behave at the dance. For us it meant bowing. Curtsying. Dancing boy-girl with hands touching. Sweaty, cookie-crumby hands. I shuddered.

For me, the sixth-grade dance meant trying to match steps with boys I'd slugged. Boys I'd said "Your mama" to in the school yard because they'd said it to me first in a battle of the Dozens. For me, and me alone, it meant waiting to be asked to dance when no one would ask because they'd have to look *way* up at me and now I was even taller than when I'd left for Oakland.

I surely didn't want to be the girl no one asked to dance. I didn't want to be the girl who swayed by the punch bowl and cookie table, pretending to enjoy watching everyone else dance. I didn't want to be Miss Merriam Webster's definition of a sixth-grade wallflower.

Those thoughts and pictures kept flashing before me.

Then Big Ma snorted. I remembered where I was. Sitting in the backseat of the Wildcat, awaiting a whipping. Only then did the pictures of the sixth-grade dance cloud and fade. June was far, far away.

Driving down Atlantic Avenue was almost as good as being home. When I was younger than Fern, I worried the Atlantic Avenue El train above us would come crashing down—trains, tracks, and all. Now I looked up and saw steel as strong as it was old. I heard and saw the sturdy old El, the train shooting across Brooklyn. The sounds above felt familiar. A few sparks jumped out beneath the train as it roared and rumbled overhead, and I made a wish on those lucky train sparks.

We were back in Bed-Stuy. The redbrick armory stood in the distance on Bedford and Atlantic Avenues like a fortress, or as Uncle Darnell would tell us, like a princess's castle. The Wildcat turned down Schenectady and again on Herkimer Street. It all looked good and welcoming. St. John's Hospital, Friendship Baptist, our elementary school, the big old softball stadium. We passed by the People's Bank—which was nothing at all like the People's Center in Oakland. We passed by burned-out buildings and weedy, littered vacant lots. Although the neighborhood begged for *Change, Positive Change* on every other election billboard after the riots, I was glad to find everything where we had left it. Even neighbors sat on their stoops as if they hadn't moved since we had gone.

Herkimer Street. Good old Herkimer Street. I was glad to be home, but I dreaded it all the same. Big Ma wasn't the kind to fall back on a promise, and she had promised me a whipping. I'd have to yelp and cry to satisfy Big Ma that I had learned my lesson. Worst of all, I'd have to put up with Vonetta's and Fern's teasing afterward. Maybe there'd still be some Oakland left in us, and my sisters would show me some solidarity, like when they gathered around me and Fern held my hand at the airport.

Pa stopped whistling "My Girl." We pulled into our driveway, and when Pa hit the brakes, the Wildcat lurched forward sharply enough to wake the nappers. Among rows of brown-brick homes, all standing together like gingerbread houses surrounded by black, spiked, iron fencing, I knew our house was odd. Not odd in the way Cecile's green, prickly stucco house was odd in Oakland. Our house was odd because the gingerbread houses stood in their own brown-brick solidarity, and our house stood apart, made from brick, stone, and siding. Whatever Pa could turn into a house. With Uncle D's help, he'd nearly built it from scratch. If anything broke down or needed fixing, he'd sigh and talk about the house like it was some old soul he'd been knowing over the years. He'd tell me how he was barely twenty and could have bought a two-year-old Thunderbird that ran like the wind, but ended up getting the lot with the burned-out frame of a house at the city auction. He'd tell me—but not Vonetta and Fern— "I was thinking of you and your sisters before I knew you'd be born."

When we got the suitcases in the house, Pa put his arms around Big Ma and spoke low in her ear. She pushed him away, saying, "This is the ruin of all things."

Pa, who had been sweet, became firm and said, "Ma.

Not on their first day home."

"Ruin," Big Ma said, although clearly Pa had won. Big Ma creaked along into the recesses of the house. She peeled off her hat and wig as she went. "Spare not. Spoil not."

"Beat not," Vonetta said as soon as Big Ma was safely out of earshot.

"Surely not."

Heckle and Jeckle

"We should let Cecile know we're here," I said.

"Back in Brooklyn," Vonetta said.

"On Herkimer Street," Fern said.

"Too bad she doesn't have a phone," I reminded my sisters.

"Or a television," Fern said.

"Or a deluxe stereo like ours, with a record player," Vonetta said. "Too, too bad."

Then it came to me, and I rapped my knuckles on top of the largest suitcase. "We've got something." I pushed open the suitcase latches while the two of them bounced on Fern's bed and asked, "What? What?" I made a mess of our folded summer clothes until I found it. A Chinatown

29

postcard of a parade dragon from our San Francisco excursion. "We can drop it in the mailbox."

"But that's our souvenir," Vonetta protested.

"For show-and-tell."

Vonetta's arms folded. "We don't want to send it."

Fern also folded her arms. "Surely don't."

I didn't entirely blame them. Cecile didn't wrap her arms around us when we first arrived, but when we hugged her good-bye, she hugged us back like she didn't want to let go. That was reason enough to send her our only souvenir, whether Vonetta and Fern liked it or not.

"She'll worry about us," I told them.

"She will not," Vonetta said.

"Yes, she will," Fern decided, and that was all I needed. To have one sister on my side. I would've sent the postcard anyway, but things went better when both thought they had an equal say.

"You know she'll worry," I told Vonetta. Truthfully I *hoped* she'd worry about us. With Cecile, you just didn't know for sure.

Vonetta gave in.

"Before we send it," I said, "we should work out what we're going to write. How about, 'Dear Cecile . . .'" I left room for my sisters to join in.

"No," Vonetta said, cutting off our rat-a-tat-tat flow before we could get it going. "We should start it with, 'Dear Mom.'"

Fern went, "P-tooey, p-tooey, p-tooey."

I agreed with Fern's fake spitting. Cecile was our mother but she wasn't a "Mom" or "Mommy." She wasn't even a "Ma" or "Mama."

"Okay, okay." Vonetta was hurt by our rejection but deep down she knew Cecile wouldn't like that "Mom" stuff. "Mom" was a TV mom, and Cecile wasn't like any mom on television.

Vonetta cleared her throat as if she were onstage at the Black Panther rally. "How about 'Dear Sister Nzila'? Yeah! 'Dear Sister Nzila, Poet of . . .'"

"The people! The people," Fern cried. "'Dear Sister Nzila, poet *to* the people.'"

"That's good!" Vonetta said. "*Poet* to the people instead of *power* to the people."

Vonetta and Fern were back in the flow of things, but I refused to write. My best handwriting was fine but large lettered. I'd never fit all of their Heckle and Jeckling on the back of our small postcard.

"Equal say" hit a pothole. How could "equal say" work when there were three of us and one small postcard? So I did what I always do. I took over.

"She knows who she is," I said in Papa's firm voice. "Instead we'll write, 'Dear Cecile,' because that's what we call her. 'We're back in Brooklyn, safe and sound on Herkimer Street. Sincerely, Delphine, Vonetta, and Fern.' That says it all and there's enough room for her

31

address and our return address."

"Boring," Vonetta said, adding a yawn to make her point. "It should be, 'We're back in Brooklyn, safe and sound . . .'"

"Not in the lost-and-found," Fern added.

Heckle rolled her eyes and shook her head. "It's 'safe and sound on the ground.'"

Then it was Jeckle's turn to yawn and say, "Boring. 'Lost-and-found' is better than 'safe and sound.'" Ever since the Black Panther rally, Fern was becoming a regular wordster, finding rhymes and soundalikes every chance she got. Miss Merriam Webster would have been proud.

"We weren't lost," Vonetta argued.

"But Big Ma found us."

"Nuh-unh. We found her. Then Delphine knocked the white man down."

"I didn't knock that man down," I said. "I bumped into him by accident, and his newspaper flew out of his hands."

Fern's eyes became big. "We should say, 'and Big Ma slapped Delphine.'"

"No, we shouldn't," I said.

"We surely should," Fern said.

Finally, we agreed to keep our postcard to our mother simple. No rhyming. No telling about the white man and his newspaper in the airport. No telling our scary, crazy mother about Big Ma's quick right hand. And to myself I said, No telling about finding a brand-new Pa who whistled Temptations songs and smelled like a Christmas tree. Heckle and Jeckle hadn't noticed anything new about Pa. They were just glad to sugar him up.

I wrote:

> *Dear Cecile,*
>
> *We are back in Brooklyn, safe and sound. We miss you.*
>
> *From,*
> *Delphine,*
> *Vonetta,*
> *and*
> *Little Girl*

I made the mistake of handing over the pen to let them sign their own names. Vonetta wrote as large as she could, then Fern decided to go back to "Little Girl," the name she wouldn't answer to in Oakland. Jeckle thought that was funny.

My Darling Daughters

We raced to the mailbox, although it wasn't much of a contest. I came in first, long-legged as I am, and Vonetta second. She kangaroo-hopped and waved her fists above her head like she had won a prize fight. Vonetta and I waited for Fern, who held the postcard. I'd put it in her hand for that reason. We couldn't do a thing without that postcard. All this to soothe Fern's wounded feelings from always coming in dead last. She panted hard when she reached us.

"Let me put it in," Vonetta said.

"No," Fern said between gulps of air. "I'm the mail carrier, so I get to put it in the mailbox."

"But I beat you to the mailbox."

I swiped the postcard clean from Fern's hand and gave it to Vonetta. Fern balled her fist and socked me, and I said, "Ow," just to say "ow." Vonetta dropped the postcard into the mailbox, then hopped and danced until Fern yelled, "Quit it!" I'm usually good at staying one step ahead of a major squabble, but my sisters seemed to have gotten better at keeping things stirred up between them.

We started back to our house in time to see Pa shuffling down the steps—and Papa's no shuffler. Vonetta and Fern ran to him like nipping puppies. I lagged behind.

"Where you going, Pa?"

"Yeah, Papa. Where?"

Pa gave both a pat on the head and said, "Out."

"Out where?" Fern asked. Only Fern could get away with tugging on Pa like that, although I also wanted to know. We had been gone from him for so long. Why was he leaving us?

This was the part where Pa was supposed to scold Fern for getting into grown folk's business. Instead, he let out a sigh and said, "Sit down, girls. Sit here on this stoop."

We sat. Each of us folded our hands in our laps, eager for whatever he was going to tell us. It was a treat to see our father on a weekday with the sun still shining. Even though we all lived under the same roof, we treasured every minute spent with Papa.

"My darling daughters," he began as if he were running for president. But that was all he said.

35

I was used to my father's quiet ways. He was as quiet as Vonetta was chatty. When he needed to say something he'd pour it out as warm as tap water. He sometimes spoke in stories when I sat with him late in the night as he ate his supper. I loved my times with Papa more than I loved the stories he told. Truth be told, Uncle Darnell was the real storyteller.

Only a few seconds had passed, but waiting for him to speak was hard on me. There was something about this new Papa. Something I couldn't figure about this father who, out of nowhere, whistled a tune other than "Old Man River."

I could smell his shaving cream and whatever else he wore. Woodsy, like he had put more of it on.

His voice cracked, but before he could pour out any words, Big Ma, who had been fanning herself before the open window, called out, "Your Pa is keeping company with a woman in Brownsville."

Pa closed his eyes. "Ma . . ."

"Ma, nothing," she said.

Fern looked to me and I said, "Pa has a lady friend," as hard and odd as it was to say those words.

Vonetta had no trouble with the whole idea. "Pa's got a girlfriend!"

Fern sang along. "Pa's got a girlfriend."

"Is that why you're whistling the Temptations?" I asked.

"And wearing perfume?" Fern asked.

36

"That's men's cologne," Pa corrected her right away.

"I'll bet she wears perfume," Vonetta sang.

"And lipstick," Fern sang with her. Then the two of them made kissing smacks.

"All right, all right," Pa said. "That's enough of that."

Pa realized I hadn't spoken up. He beamed at me, waiting. I looked at the ground.

"Her name is Marva Hendrix. And I'd like you all to meet her."

When I glanced up, I saw dimples. My father had dimples like Uncle Darnell's. I'd never noticed them before. I looked back down.

Fern said right away, "Marva. Rhymes with larva."

Then Vonetta couldn't let it be, and added, "And George Washington Carver." And while they argued if Carver rhymed with larva, I saw pictures of my Temptations-whistling, dimpled, smiling father sitting in the RKO movie theater munching on popcorn with his arm around Miss Marva Hendrix's shoulders. This wasn't the kind of picture you're supposed to have of your father while your sisters made kissing smacks. My papa was thirty-two and acting like a teenager. The hippies were right. You can't trust anyone over thirty.

Big Ma's dinner should have tasted like the meal of a lifetime, but how could it when there were two empty places at dinner? Pa was out keeping company with a Miss Marva

37

Hendrix from Brownsville, and Uncle Darnell was carrying a rifle in the jungles of Vietnam.

My sisters didn't have any problem lifting their forks. They ate and entertained Big Ma and told more than we'd agreed on about our time with Cecile. Thank goodness Big Ma was in a talking mood instead of a whipping mood. "Nothing but a piss-pot of boiling trouble," Big Ma said. "I told him not to send you. I told him." Only when she started in on Cecile did my sisters feel bad for telling all that they told.

"My son, my son," Big Ma said. "He can pick 'em. I'll say that."

My appetite never did catch up to me, although my sisters' spoons dived happily into their 'nana pudding. I got up and took a few dishes into the kitchen to wash. My Timex was waterproof, but I laid it on the counter while Vonetta and Fern fought over my untouched dessert.

P.S. Be Eleven

It took one week and one day before we heard from Cecile. Leave it to our mother to make her own postcard. As grand and sturdy as a birthday card.

Big Ma got it first, along with the rest of the mail. I stopped dusting when she hollered, "What in the world?" I was all eyes and ears; my heart was skipping rope. Cecile's movable-type letters were bold enough to be seen from down the hall. I sped into the living room where Big Ma sat, going through the mail.

"Is that for us?" I asked.

She was reading it. Cecile's card. I couldn't tell if she had scrunched up her face from reading what Cecile had written or from turning up her nose at Cecile's movable-type letters in red, black, and green. She read the card and gave a "Hmph." Instead of handing it to me, Big Ma dropped the postcard on the table like it was nothing. "Come get it if you want it."

You'd think I'd be angry that Big Ma violated our right to privacy and read our postcard. All the rights my sisters and I had been filled with only existed at the People's Center or out of the mouths of Black Panthers. We were back on Herkimer Street under Big Ma, and we had to keep most of what we learned in Oakland to ourselves.

I yelled, "Vonetta! Fern!" They raced into the living room. "Guess what came!" I held up the postcard so they could see the lettering.

They shouted, "Cecile!" and a lot of "Lemme sees." I handed the card over to Vonetta, who did the honors and read the poem out loud in her poetry-reciting voice. While Vonetta recited, Fern did the dance that told of the summer leaves falling into color, falling away and then breaking through spring branches. Fern twirled to the part about leaves always coming back but in different shades. Then she went spring-leafy crazy on the buds-breaking-through-branches part, and Vonetta had to join her.

Big Ma called it beatnik nonsense.

Vonetta cleared her voice to make it deeper and read

the letter part in her Cecile voice:

"'Dear Delphine, Vonetta, and Fern . . . ,'"

"She said 'Fern'!" Fern squealed.

"Little Girl," Vonetta kept it up in her Cecile voice, "I am blowing dust off your mind. Do not interrupt the great Nzila." She cleared her throat and went on. It was all a funny joke to us that Big Ma didn't get, and for a moment my grandmother not liking my mother hurt like a dull toothache.

I'm glad you're all safe.
Everyone here says hello.
Write back if you want to.
Your Mother.
Cecile.

"I'm going to write," I said.

"Me too," Fern said.

"Okay. Me too," Vonetta said in her own voice. "If you're writing, I'm writing."

Vonetta and Fern fussed over the card until they almost tore it, so I took it away.

"Everyone in Oakland said hello," I said. "At least they haven't forgotten us."

Vonetta fluttered her eyelashes and said, "You mean, at least Hirohito hasn't forgotten you."

41

"Hurraheeto? Hurraheeto?" Big Ma asked. "What's a Hurraheeto?"

"Delphine's boyfriend," Vonetta said.

"Only ten and starting this mess already," Big Ma said. "A mercy."

"He's not my boyfriend," I said, but he was the closest person to a boyfriend I'd ever had. Besides my father and Uncle D. "And I'm eleven."

"Ten. 'Leven. Same difference," Big Ma said. "And what kind of ooga-mooga name is Hurraheeto?"

"It's not ooga mooga, Big Ma," Fern said, which we all knew was Big Ma's way of saying African. But she also called "Vonetta" and "Delphine" ooga-mooga names because they came from Cecile's imagination, when only Fern's name, Afua, was a true ooga-mooga name. I guessed that was why Afua was not on Fern's birth certificate or school papers. Big Ma had no use for anything African. Pa probably felt the same way.

"It's Japanese," Vonetta said. "And his last name is black. Hirohito Woods."

"Woods is not a black last name," I said.

"Charlene Woods in my class is black. Her brother, Delroy Woods, is black."

I probably had a "Cecile look" on my face for the times we said things that completely confounded her. I didn't even know where to begin with Vonetta's thinking.

42

Fern explained Hirohito to Big Ma. "He's Japaneezy looking and black."

Big Ma gave another hmph. "War baby." Both what she said and how she said it might as well have been street talk that Big Ma or Papa didn't allow in this house. But how did you correct someone who brought you into the world and held a strap to you?

"His mother is Japanese and his father is black," I explained.

"And in jail," Vonetta volunteered. I glared at her.

"Jail?" Big Ma was horrified. "That Hurraheeto's father's in jail? A mercy, a mercy. Shoulda never let y'all board that plane."

"He's a political prisoner," I said. "Unjustly incarcerated by the Man." Now I was speaking like Crazy Kelvin. Crazy Kelvin, the strongest-speaking Black Panther my sisters and I had met at the People's Center, who was also shown up to be a phony. An infiltrator. Just a plain traitor.

"You can't tell me nothing about that war baby's father. He's 'bout criminal. Just like the rest of 'em. Nothing but a band of criminals leading good Negroes astray."

Fern only heard "war baby" and thought that was a good thing. "War baby!" she said.

"Uncle Darnell's in a war," Vonetta said. "I'll bet he has a war baby."

"Ooh!" Fern cried. "I get to dress her."

"It could be a boy," Vonetta said. "We'll take turns."

"Will y'all stop this nonsense?" Big Ma said. "Uncle Darnell ain't bringing no war babies home from Vietnam."

"Shuck corn," Vonetta said.

"Yeah. Shucks."

I asked Big Ma for two dollars to buy first-class envelopes, a memo pad, and postage stamps so we could write a proper letter to our mother. And to my pen pal, Hirohito, but I kept that to myself. My sisters walked with me to the candy store around the corner on Fulton. They were more interested in leftover change for Jolly Ranchers candy than in stationery and stamps. When we returned home, I gave them each two pieces of candy and I began my letters.

Dear Hirohito,

How are you? I am fine.

I didn't know what else to write or where to send his letter. We said we would write to each other, but I didn't give him my address in Brooklyn and I forgot to get his address in Oakland.

I did know what to say to my mother and where to send her letter.

Dear Cecile,

How are you? I am fine.

I had to write this letter now because I need to know something and you don't have a telephone.

Did you love my father? Did he love you? Do you miss my father like he missed you?

I'm asking because Pa has a lady friend who lives in Brownsville. He told us her name and he takes her out on dates like a teenager when he is our father.

If you still have feelings for our father, he might forget all about this lady in Brownsville.

Vonetta, Fern, and I really liked your postcard.

Yours truly,
Delphine

P.S. Please say hello to everyone for me.

I received Cecile's letter by airmail, nine days later.

Dear Delphine,

The green stucco house is mine, bought and paid for. Mine to stucco and paint. Mine to live in.
The sofa I sleep on, the books stacked on the floor, are mine. Not all the clothes are rightfully mine, but I

feel I have a right to them too. Like I've paid for them although I didn't lay out a cent to wear them. They are still paid for. They are mine and no one else's. They've conformed to me and can't be worn by anyone but me. The palm tree in my yard is mine. Someone got tired of it, or grew disappointed with it and threw it out. I brought it home, dug a hole on the side of the house, and planted it where it would get sun. The palm tree tries to stand up because someone wants it. It knows it is wanted. It knows it is mine.

The printer is mine. It was left out for scrap. It was heavy and in pieces, but I lifted it. Got it on the bus. Worked on it and worked on it until I got the rollers to turn and the gears to turn. No one carried it and fixed it but me. It is mine.

My feelings about your father are mine. They are not feelings that can be understood by a young girl. They are my feelings. Mine.

Don't worry about these things. Study hard. Have your own things.

Your Mother.
Cecile

P.S. Be eleven.

Meeting Miss Hendrix

Things were back to normal—if Pa whistling was normal. Big Ma fell asleep in her chair during *Peyton Place*, with a movie-star newspaper in her lap underneath her Bible. I mopped the kitchen floor. My sisters took their baths.

I got used to Pa's new face and whistling. That he worked from early morning and was home in time for supper most days. No more working all day and all night for Pa. No more long, tired faces.

It was all because of Miss Marva Hendrix, his lady friend in Brownsville on the other side of Atlantic Avenue. I should have been glad my father's dimples showed when he smiled and that he wasn't tired from working day and night. I should have been glad my father had a spring in his step and took his new shirts to the cleaners. I should have danced a jig and said, "Less shirts for me to wash, wring out, starch, and iron." If Pa was happy, then I should have been happy too. But I wasn't.

One night after dinner, Pa said, "I think it's time you met Marva. Yes. The time has come." He had used the same voice and the same words to tell us we were flying to Oakland to reunite with our mother. He'd said it was a thing whose time had come.

When he spoke those words about meeting Cecile, he was long-faced and serious. When he said them about Miss Marva Hendrix, he was lighthearted and ready for some teasing—at least from Vonetta and Fern. I tried to not be an old, wet sock, but I didn't feel like teasing. I felt like time had come too soon.

Before I could properly sulk about it, the doorbell rang and Pa was smiling and springing up out of his chair. Vonetta and Fern tap-danced in their tennis shoes until Big Ma warned them to stop acting like a bunch of untrained chimps and to not shame Pa.

He brought his lady friend inside like how the church ushers brought a visiting guest to the special pew up front.

Miss Marva Hendrix was what magazines called petite. Her Afro was Angela Davis big, but curly like she'd spent a lot of time rolling it up the night before and picking it out. Her dress and shoes were snappy and mod, like Miss

Honeywell's, my soon-to-be sixth-grade teacher. She wore eye shadow—too light and bright for her skin coloring, in my opinion. Her lashes were coated with mascara, and her eyebrows were thick but plucked to form a steep *"I see . . ."* arch. Her nails were icy blue like her eye shadow. Miss Marva Hendrix was everything my mother wasn't.

Big Ma and I must have thought the same thing: Miss Marva Hendrix was almost out of a fashion magazine. No wonder my father wore brand-new shirts that he only trusted with the cleaners.

I didn't like her before I'd seen her. Now that I saw her, nothing had changed.

"Mama, darling daughters—"

This got an eye roll from Big Ma.

"I'd like you to meet . . ."

Heckle and Jeckle giggled and shook and I wished they'd be still. After not having a mother for so long, we had finally met and hugged our mother and lived in her house and said her poetry and cleaned up her kitchen and gathered up her papers and her movable-type pieces after the police messed up her work space. We had just met, hugged, and maybe even loved our mother, smelled the coconut oil in her big braids, and there my sisters were, wiggling like worms in a bait box.

"Miss Marva Hendrix," Pa said proudly.

I knew better than to cross my arms and roll my eyes. I knew better but I couldn't help myself. My forearms

49

bolted across my chest, each hand clamped fast around my arm muscles. I at least had enough sense to *not* roll my eyes. I said, "Nice to meet you, Miss Hendrix."

"Marva," she offered.

"Miss Marva Hendrix," I said. Big Ma's firm nod told me to not forget my home training no matter what Pa's lady friend said.

"That's Delphine, my oldest," Pa said, although looking at us, there was no need to offer that open-faced fact. "This is—"

Vonetta shot up, curtsied, and said in her best showy and crowy voice, "I'm Vonetta. The middle!"

Fern did Vonetta one better, daintily holding out her skirt hem as if she wore a hoopskirt, and said, "I'm Fern, but my mother calls me Afua." She curtsied on the "Afua."

Miss Hendrix smiled and nodded, a kind of a bow to Fern's curtsy. "Which do you prefer, Fern or Afua?"

"You can call me Fern." Then she added, "Only my mother calls me Afua."

I envied my baby sister. I wished I could just say things. Did she know she had just told Pa's lady friend that she was not her mother?

Miss Marva Hendrix didn't seem to mind. Perhaps it was that Fern was still little and sweet-voiced. Her eyes were bright and aimed to please. Big Ma, however, was none-too-pleased by Fern owning up to her ooga-mooga name. But Fern's words had given me a spark, and I felt a little better.

Miss Marva Hendrix tugged at Pa's shirt, looked up at him while batting her heavy eyelashes, and said, "No time like the present, Lou." Her voice was singsongy, but I could hear her *telling* my father. Not asking.

Pa seemed to agree. He smiled at her, turned to Big Ma, and said, "Ma." Then he said, "Girls," and turned to each of us. Me first, Vonetta, and then Fern. "I've asked Marva to be my wife."

Vonetta and Fern squealed. Big Ma put on a polite smile. My father's words ran through me like something I shouldn't have eaten. I felt weak down to my toes and warm all over. Somehow, I managed to do like Big Ma. I put on a polite smile and said, "That's nice, Papa." I didn't know what else to say.

What else do you say when your father announces he's getting married? What do you say when you don't like his lady friend—can't possibly ever like her—but you don't dare shame your Pa, Big Ma, or, as Big Ma would say, "all the Charleses, Gaithers, and Trotters in Prattville, Alabama." What can you do when your lip has dropped into a mile-long pout while everyone else is happy, or at least being polite? You put on a smile and say it again. "That's nice, Pa. Very nice," because none of Miss Merriam Webster's words will show up in time to save you. You remember how Mrs. Peterson forbade the use of the word *very* in book reports because *very* was fine for fourth graders, but too lazy for fifth graders. Yet here you are, getting ready to start the sixth grade using fourth-grade words. You can't help yourself and add another *very*. "Very, very nice, Papa."

"You asked her to be your wife?" Vonetta asked. "What did she say?"

It was clear to me, but Fern asked, "Will she?"

Miss Marva Hendrix extended her hand to show the two white stones on her ring finger. "I told your father I will."

Big Ma said, "My. Isn't that pretty." She was still being polite. Good old Big Ma.

Vonetta and Fern started another bout of squealing. My old Papa would have reeled in their noise. My new Papa let Vonetta's and Fern's excitement run wild. New Pa bent down and gave Miss Hendrix a smack on the lips to encourage Vonetta and Fern, who obliged him with a lot of high-pitched oohing. Then Big Ma told Pa and his lady friend, "That's enough of that. You're not married yet." Even so, she said to Miss Hendrix, "Welcome to the family, Marva dear," as nicely as she could, but she didn't give her a big hug.

Later that night when were all sitting on my bed, Vonetta announced, "I'm the flower girl."

"Me too!" Fern cried.

"I called it first!"

"But I'm younger and shorter and you're too big, you big fourth grader."

I stared at them in Cecile-like disbelief. How could my own sisters go on and on about being flower girls, wearing pink satin dresses, and getting their hair pressed and curled for Papa's wedding to another woman? How could they fight over Cecile's postcard one day and throw their mother away without a care the next day?

Soon enough, my sisters' wedding plans turned to arguing over how to throw rose petals. I couldn't take another word of it. "Y'all need to quit it," I said. "Pa and Miss Hendrix are too old to have a fairy-tale wedding with flower girls and harps playing."

But Fern heard harps playing. She ballet-teetered on her toes to the harp strings plucking in her head, and Vonetta joined her, twirling and leaping. I watched my own sisters through my mother's eyes, happily dancing this woman into our house.

To and fRom Cecile

Vonetta wrote:

Dear Cecile,

How are you? I am fine. Delphine made us write "Dear Cecile" but this is my letter and I can write what I want. Which do you like best? Mother? Mommy? How about Little Ma, since we already have Big Ma? Since you are bigger than Big Ma, I'll just write Cecile. Remember I said I'm going into the fourth grade? In two weeks I'll be in my fourth-grade classroom. My new teacher's name is Mrs. Dixon. I'll tell her you're my mother and Big Ma is my grandmother because she'll see Big Ma at the parent-teacher confrens and she won't see you.

Pa is getting married to a nice lady with groovy makeup and clothes. I'm going to be the flower girl. I will look pretty in my flower girl dress. I want my dress to be yellow, pink, or violet.

Delphine is a giant crab.

Yours truly,
Vonetta Gaither

Fern wrote:

To Nzila

I like leaves in the summer.
I like leaves in the fall.
There's no leaves in the winter.
So don't leave

Afua.

She made the first *A* in Afua extra large and the small *a* with a curly tail to match the way Cecile signs her poems in movable-type printing blocks. A large and fancy *N* and a fancy *z* with a tail.

I said, "Fern, you forgot the period."

She pointed to the one after her name and said, "There it is."

I pointed to the word *leave*. "It goes there. After 'don't leave.'"

She said, "No, it doesn't."

I said, "It's wrong, Fern."

She bobbed her little turtle head and snapped, "It's right so don't touch it."

"Fine," I said. "Send it that way."

"I'm sending it that way, and you better not touch it." She folded her arms, happy to be wrong.

I checked Vonetta's letter and rolled my eyes about the "giant crab" part.

"You shouldn't write all of this stuff about Cecile being big and how that lady Pa's marrying is nice."

"Cecile is big. Bigger than Big Ma. Bigger than you," Vonetta said. "And Pa's fiancée is nice and wears nice clothes."

"Surely is. Surely does."

"That still doesn't mean you should write it," I said. How could she use that word? *Fiancée. Pa's fiancée.*

"You can't tell us what to write. We have the freedom to write what we want."

"And to put a period where we want to."

"And to say Miss Hendrix is nice."

"Power to the people."

"Power to the people, *right on.*"

I wanted to write a letter to Hirohito but I didn't know his house number. If I took a guess and sent it, and the post office returned it, Big Ma would get my letter first. She'd probably open it and read it and tell me I was too young to be writing to a boy.

I decided to write to my mother instead. Cecile had already told me to mind my business about her feelings and about Pa, but I still wanted to know why my parents didn't get married. Why my father bought Miss Marva Hendrix a ring but he didn't buy one for my mother.

Instead, I told Cecile how I tried to help Vonetta and Fern with their letters but they didn't want my help. I said Vonetta and Fern were driving me crazy and that I couldn't wait for school to start so I could officially be in the sixth grade.

I didn't ask her for Hirohito's address like I wanted to. She'd make a big federal case out of it like Big Ma had and write back and say things that made me feel bad or want to scratch my head. I just closed my letter with "Yours truly" and my name.

If Cecile cared where Fern put her period and if Papa's lady friend was nice, or if Vonetta planned on being a flower girl, she didn't mention it in her letter to me. When the envelope with an Oakland, California, postmark arrived, I opened it and gave Vonetta her letter and Fern hers. I thought they would read their letters out loud, but they took them and ran back to their room.

To me she wrote:

Dear Delphine,

You all have something. I saw it at the rally. Vonetta is a natural-born performer. She can open her mouth and holler when she wants to.
That Little Girl is a natural-born poet. You saw her being born on the kitchen floor, and I saw a poet being born up on that stage. Her rally poem isn't exactly Longfellow but it is a running start. She might run far. Let her go. Let her run.
Don't concern yourself with old things. Concern your-self with finding your own thing. But don't rush. Listen to Billie sing, "God bless the child who has her own." Enjoy the time it takes to find your own.
Study hard.

Your Mother.
Cecile

P.S. Be eleven.

She'd written it again. "P.S. Be eleven."

I stared at it like it was the wrong grade marked on the bottom of my paper. My mother was a touch crazy, not dumb. But now I felt dumb because I didn't know Billie or why Cecile had written that twice. "P.S. Be eleven."

I *was* eleven. How could you become what you already were?

School Shopping

"Big Ma, please."

I'm no pleader or whiner, but I found myself making those sounds at Big Ma in Korvettes department store on school shopping day. Big Ma kept pulling hangers of pleated wool skirts off the rack and putting them back. She paid me no mind. I still hoped she had heard me.

"Can I just try on—"

"You'll try what I give you. Now hush, Delphine."

Vonetta and Fern stuck their tongues out at me.

I was tired of wearing the same pleated wool skirts my sisters wore, but Big Ma wouldn't hear about anything different. According to Big Ma, we should look like we were prepared to sit at our desks at school and not to dig ditches in the dirt. Pants-wearers dug ditches, and no female should wear any pants other than underpants. The only exceptions were shorts with matching tops for summertime running around. According to Big Ma, pants were a man's business and no woman had any business in them.

My mother wore pants. Men's pants.

It's not that I wanted them. I didn't. I knew better than to ask for a pair of bell-bottoms or jeans, although Miss Honeywell looked snappy and mod in her shocking-pink bell-bottom pants and matching jacket with big gold buttons. It was all the school talked about. Miss Honeywell, a teacher and a grown woman, was escorted to the principal's office like a bad boy walking the "paddle mile," while a hallway aide watched her classroom. My soon-to-be teacher wasn't sent home to change clothes, but she never wore her shocking-pink pantsuit or any other pants to school again.

All I wanted was to start the sixth grade with a sixth-grade look. I wanted to pick out my own skirts and jumpers. I didn't care that we shopped at Korvettes and not at Macy's or Gertz. I only wanted to have a say in what I looked like.

Big Ma had picked out three skirts each for Vonetta and Fern in the children's department, and now it was my turn. Nothing Big Ma held up to me had a prayer of fitting.

"Dag nabbit!" Big Ma never swore, but she did that day. Skirt after skirt failed, and Big Ma let loose another "dag nabbit."

It was a sign. A sign from above. My long arms and legs were good for something. Maybe even part of His plan to come to my rescue.

We were now forced to shop among the junior miss racks. I had a better chance of picking out my own clothes. And if I didn't, I'd at least look mod, although I'd have been happy just to look normal.

Big Ma must have prayed harder to find wool pleated skirts, because among all those mod new jumpers and skirts, she managed to find a rack of babyish pleated skirts. She held one up to me. The hem fell at least five inches below my knee. I would start off the sixth grade looking like a schoolmarm on *Gunsmoke*.

Please. Please, I prayed. If Big Ma wouldn't listen, maybe the Lord would.

I was tired of staring down every other girl in my grade who snickered at my pleated wool skirts and Peter Pan collars. All I wanted was to look like everyone else. Wasn't fighting with immature boys in the school yard more than enough to bear?

I focused my eyes away from inward prayer only to zero in on Lucy Raleigh, Miss Everyone Else, shopping at Korvettes with her mother. How could a prayer go so wrong? I must have stood out like a giraffe because she saw me before I could turn away. Mrs. Raleigh called after her, her arms laden with outfits—all mod, I was certain. Lucy ignored her mother and charged our way. You'd have thought Lucy would have been ashamed to be caught shopping in Korvettes when she bragged her clothes came from Macy's and Gertz. Yet, there she was doing the opposite of shrinking and fleeing.

Lucy Raleigh was one of my oldest friends, but she could also snicker at me with the best of the snickerers. We ran hot, warm, and cold with each other. I always adjusted my friendliness to meet hers.

When she made it over, Fern sang, "Luceee, Lucee goosey." Lucy thought Fern's song was cute and danced to it, and Vonetta had to get in on the Lucy Goosey dance too. Big Ma didn't appreciate any of this finger popping and making a grand Negro spectacle of ourselves in the junior miss section of Korvettes department store.

Big Ma's disdain bounced right off of Lucy. In fact, Lucy was loud and gushy, and she was never too gushy with me. "You're back! You're back!" she said. "Hi, Mrs. Gaither. Nice hat. Jazzy feather."

Lucy Raleigh always managed to rub Big Ma the wrong way. She once called Lucy my "some-timey friend," meaning Lucy wasn't true-blue.

Lucy reached into a rack and pulled out a mod jumper and said, "Get this," and shoved it at Big Ma until she had no choice but to take it. Lucy then squeezed my hand

and led me away from my grandmother and sisters. I was bigger and stronger than Lucy, but I allowed myself to be pulled away.

Lucy held both my hands and jumped small "testifying before the altar" jumps. "Turn on channel seven and watch *The Hollywood Palace* tonight."

"Why?" I asked her. It was something big. Something important. Lucy Raleigh liked being the one in the know and I couldn't pretend I didn't care.

"Because if you don't, you'll kick yourself from Sunday to Monday and back to Sunday. I'm telling you, Miss Too Cool to Keep Up. You have to watch it. You *and* your sisters."

"Why can't you tell me who's going to be on?" I asked. "What's so special? And why do they have to see it too?"

"I told you. If you miss it, you'll die. And if they miss it, they'll want to kill you."

We might have been whispering for a minute but it was a minute too long for Mrs. Raleigh.

"Girl, I'm 'bout to leave these clothes and you in here if you don't come on. What do you mean, running off, Lucy Ray?"

I giggled a little. Lucy liked to put on how she was all Brooklyn when her mother was as country as Big Ma.

"Coming, Mama," Lucy said, rushing back to her. She turned to me and said, "Channel seven. *Hollywood Palace.* Tonight!"

I had my own grandmother to face. She settled on two pleated skirts for me but hadn't put back the jumper Lucy had shoved in her hands. I got an earful from Big Ma, but she paid for the mod jumper.

Prayer works.

I Want You Back

One thing was certain. Lucy Raleigh didn't have a bed-time like my sisters and me. Vonetta and Fern had to be bathed, in pj's, and in bed by eight thirty. My bedtime was nine o'clock or after I finished reading them a bed-time story, scrubbing their tub, and taking my own bath. Since Big Ma counted on me to look after my sisters, my bedtime began to shift and slide past nine. I'd sit qui-etly on the rug watching an episode of *The FBI* that Big Ma had fallen asleep on. Even after I climbed in bed I'd sleep lightly enough to hear my father's keys jingling at the door around midnight, and I'd go warm up his food.

I didn't know how much longer past eight thirty my sisters could stay awake, but for once I'd listen to Lucy

Raleigh. I told Vonetta and Fern we had to watch something on TV and to be ready when I came to get them.

"You have to be quiet," I told my sisters. "You can't
wake Big Ma or we'll miss it."

"Miss what? You still didn't tell us," Vonetta said.

I didn't know, but I didn't want to come off not knowing. I said, trusting Lucy Raleigh, "It's a surprise. The best
surprise. You just have to be quiet and watch." When we
got out in the hallway, I said, "We're on a spy mission. Top
secret." I zipped my lips. They did the same and followed
me into the living room.

It was half past the hour. The show was already on, and
I hoped we hadn't missed the surprise.

Big Ma snored ferociously, her body sunk peacefully
into her comfy chair.

I turned the sound all the way down and clicked the
dial to channel seven. With each click I waited for Big
Ma to awaken and send us to bed without our seeing the
surprise. Big Ma snored on.

We sat before the glowing television, careful to not
make a noise.

So far, we had seen Diana Ross without the Supremes,
wearing a glittery gold jumpsuit. Even gold came across as
gold on a black-and-white television set. I smiled to myself
and thought, Miss Diana Ross wasn't hardly digging any
ditches in her sparkly gold pants.

Before you knew it, Sammy Davis Jr. had joined her

67

on the stage and the two joked around with each other. We couldn't hear the jokes, but even if we could, I knew the two performers were not the surprise we waited for. I liked Diana Ross and the Supremes. I liked Sammy Davis Jr. in his sharp black suits, tap-dancing and singing all cool with his hair slick and shiny. If it were the afternoon on *The Mike Douglas Show*, my sisters and I would have been glued to the TV screen, shouting, "Black infinity!" because black folks were on TV for more than a minute. But it was late into the night and I had pulled my sisters out of bed on a spy mission that wasn't worth a whipping. I had put my trust in Lucy when I should have known better. After all, Lucy wasn't my best, best friend. Frieda Banks was.

I turned the sound up just a little and we moved closer to the screen. We could hear Diana Ross telling Sammy Davis Jr. something about five Jacksons and the lead singer, whose name was Michael. That was the last sane and clear thought I had before I saw at least a hundred bright lightbulbs and five boys onstage singing that new Sly and the Family Stone song. Our television screen didn't seem big enough for all those Jacksons. Afros bopping, arms swinging, and feet stepping and spinning in sync. And they wore wide bell-bottoms like crazy! The voices in the back were smooth and together. And the little boy singer let out his lungs like James Brown and

68

Jackie Wilson rolled into one.

Our mouths opened to scream, but we were on a spy mission. Vonetta and I covered our mouths with our hands. Fern stuffed the bottom of her nightie in her mouth. And we shook and silently screamed.

Then the Jackson boys had gone from singing the Sly and the Family Stone song to singing a slower song. A love song about remembering.

The camera kept showing the youngest boy, but he wasn't the one I watched. I felt myself tremble every time they showed the tallest Jackson brother. And I swore—and I didn't swear—if Big Ma was whipping my legs with her lightning strap, I wouldn't have felt a lick. I could only feel my heart beating and my eyes tearing every time they showed him on the screen. He had to be the oldest. And tall. So tall.

Every time the youngest one sang, "Can you remember?" Fern whispered, "Surely do!" We didn't bother to shush her.

The camera kept putting Michael up on the screen and that made Fern happy. Vonetta too. But I was happy to get a glimpse of the oldest one and wished he sang the love song. As tall as he was, he danced smooth. Better than all of his little brothers put together.

Then a commercial came on and we all squeezed one another and bit our hands to keep from screaming. We had to sit through the other performers, but finally it was time for the five brothers to return, and Diana Ross introduced them: The Jackson Five.

The youngest one started things off, telling us they had an album coming out, and then the piano rolled hard and the guitars twanged electric and loud and that little boy was begging his girlfriend to come back while his brothers "ooh-hoo-hooed" and Vonetta, Fern, and I screamed and danced with the Jackson Five.

Then Big Ma woke up.

"Go to bed! Y'all better get in your beds. Now."

We stopped dancing but we couldn't stop watching. We were frozen by fear of the strap and frozen by the Jackson Five and the most electric song ever played, sung, or danced to. We didn't know what to do.

"Where's my strap?" Big Ma said. "Delphine, get me my strap!"

I managed to say, "Can we see the rest, Big Ma? Can we see it?"

"Please, Big Ma."

"We gotta, gotta see it!"

"Do you know what time it is?" Big Ma asked, searching for the clock. "It's nighttime. There's nothing on TV for children this time of night."

"They're children," I answered. "They're our age." Although the oldest Jackson had to be in the eleventh or twelfth grade. And then there was the guitar player. The one with the eyebrows. He had to be in high school. And the other guitar player, too.

"That should be against the law," Big Ma said. "Children singing and dancing on TV late at night."

"Please, Big Ma. Please."

She wagged her finger at us. "This is your no-mother-of-a-mother's doing. Y'all come back here as wild as a bunch of untrained, back-talking chimps sneaking around in the night."

"Please, Big Ma. We won't ask for nothing else," I begged.

"Ever," my sisters chimed in.

But Big Ma got up out of her chair and turned off the TV set. She picked up her Bible from the end table and sat back down.

"You seen 'em. Now if those boys have any kind of mother and father, they'll snatch those children off the stage and get them home to bed. Now y'all get in your beds before your father comes home and sees you're up."

"But it's not over," Vonetta wailed.

"We want Michael," Fern said.

"Michael? Michael?" Her face was like Cecile's when we said things that made her think we were Martians, or at the very least, not her children. "What you want is my strap." It was when Big Ma lifted herself up and out of her comfy chair that we knew she wasn't just fussing with us, and we scooted back to our rooms.

I turned out my light and fell into my bed. I had never cried so hard in my life. Not because I couldn't see the rest of the show, but because I saw him, and he was tall. Taller than me.

At Madison Square Garden

The front passenger seat in the Wildcat belonged to Big Ma when the whole gang of us piled into the car. If Big Ma stayed home, Uncle Darnell sat up front next to Pa. If it was just us girls with Pa, that seat was mine, and I loved being up front, stealing glances at my pa as he hummed but didn't whistle to Otis Redding's "Sittin' on the Dock of the Bay" and, of course, to "Old Man River"—all songs that suited my old pa. Sometimes he'd pass me the smallest grin and I'd feel wonderful bumping along as the tires hit every pothole on Atlantic or Fulton Avenue on our way to wherever we were going. Vonetta would wail, "Why does *she*"—meaning me—"get to sit up front all the time?"

"And not us," Fern would chirp.

Then Pa always said, "To keep an eye on the road," as if I was really doing something when all I did was keep Pa company. I'd ride along bubbling up with things to say but I never uttered a one, which suited Pa fine. He just wanted me to be with him. That was how it was between Cecile and me when I was little and she kept me with her while she wrote poems and listened to Sarah Vaughn records on our deluxe stereo while Vonetta howled in her crib.

When Miss Hendrix bent down and slid her bottom onto the passenger seat, swinging her legs in last, I knew my days of riding up front next to Pa in the Wildcat were numbered.

"Can we go to the RKO after Central Park, Pa?" Vonetta asked.

Miss Hendrix snickered and gave Pa a playful tap. "Pa. That sounds old. And country."

Pa shrugged it off, but I didn't. I took note of everything she did and said.

We were close to the Brooklyn Bridge when Vonetta cried, "Look!"

"What?" I asked, convinced it was nothing at all. I had been staring off into the blur of Miss Marva Hendrix's curly Afro.

"Look-look!" she cried out.

And then I saw it. We all saw what Vonetta could see

from hundreds of feet away. A billboard of Jackie, Jermaine, Tito, Marlon, and Michael sporting big applejack caps over their even bigger Afros. We screamed. The letters on the billboard shouted at us: THE JACKSON FIVE AT MADISON SQUARE GARDEN. And underneath those words: DECEMBER. The inside of the Wildcat became a cage of screaming and seat-jumping until we finally heard Pa shouting, "All right! All right back there!" Miss Marva Hendrix laughed and laughed.

I screamed for Jackie, whose real name was Sigmund, and I screamed for Tito, who had the best eyebrows and always looked cool and tough. Vonetta screamed for Jermaine, who was kind of good looking, and she screamed for Marlon, whom she claimed was the best dancer. The only Jackson Fern screamed for was Michael. Every chance we got, we'd stand in the record department of Korvettes and study every inch of their album cover.

"Papa, can we go to Madison Square Garden in December?" I asked.

"To see the Jackson Five?"

"We want to see the Jackson Five."

We sealed our wishes together singing, "Pleeeease."

"The Jackson who?" Pa asked. "Sounds like a Mississippi chain gang."

Vonetta asked, "What's a chain gang?"

"They make chains," Fern answered, sounding every bit like me.

The two got to arguing about chain gangs, which I think Pa intended all along. I wouldn't let go of our wishes. If we learned anything from our summer with the Black Panthers, we learned to be clear about what we wanted, and to be willing to do what was necessary to get it.

"They are not a prison chain gang." I threw in the prison part to answer Vonetta's question and for solidarity. I needed my sisters to be united with me and to stay focused. "The Jackson Five is the best singing group in the world."

"In the universe," Vonetta added.

"And the Milky Way."

"Jackson Five?" Pa said. "Never heard of them. Can't sing better than Sam Cooke. Or the Temptations."

"And what about Smokey Robinson and the Miracles?" Miss Hendrix said. "Oh. And Marvin Gaye."

I said, "The Jackson Five are better than all of those singers and groups put together."

"Their Afros are bigger," Vonetta said.

"And they have Michael," Fern said. "He's better than best."

"He is not," I said.

"Jermaine is the best," Vonetta said.

"Jackie is the best looking," I said, "and then Tito."

"Not hardly," Vonetta said. "Jermaine is. And Marlon is the best dancer. Like I am."

And before we knew it, our solidarity had fallen apart.

For the rest of the ride to Central Park, we did nothing but argue about the Jackson Five until Fern began to sing "Can You Remember" and Vonetta and I joined her. Pa and Miss Hendrix talked amongst themselves.

We bought ginger ale and a bucket of fried chicken and we headed over to Central Park with a blanket. Big Ma wouldn't have seen the point in an outing like this. Especially buying store-fried chicken. But there we were, spending a lazy Saturday afternoon with our father, eating chicken I didn't have to cut, clean, and fry. I could put up with his lady friend tagging along.

"Papa," I said as calmly as I could, "we want to see the Jackson Five."

"At Madison Square Garden."

"In December."

All together we sang, "Pleeease."

"I don't know," Pa said. "Madison Square Garden. New York City. Mobs of screaming teenagers. I don't know."

This was a time that called for Uncle Darnell. He'd know who the Jackson Five were, and he was grown enough to take us to the Garden. Instead of Uncle Darnell coming to our rescue, Miss Hendrix said, "What if I took them?"

Vonetta and Fern began to shriek and Pa covered his ears. As much as I wanted to see Jackie and Tito in person, I refused to shriek. I didn't want anything from Pa's lady friend.

"How much could the tickets cost, sweetie?" She

fluttered her eyelashes at my father. "Five, six dollars each? And a little extra for soda? Popcorn. Raisinets. Maybe a hot dog."

My sisters screamed. Pa choked. "Marva honey. That's nearly seven or eight dollars."

All I heard was "honey."

"Are you sure you want to do that? All those rowdy teenagers screaming and hollering over some finger-popping little hoodlums in Afros?"

"They're not hoodlums!" Vonetta cried out. "They're entertainers."

"Surely are," Fern said. "They entertain us."

The "honey" stuck to me. The sick sweetness of it. I knew I had to unstick myself if I wanted to see Jackie and Tito Jackson. I decided I wanted to see them more than I didn't like Pa's lady friend.

"As long as the girls behave, there won't be a problem," Miss Marva Hendrix said.

"We'll behave," Vonetta pledged without hesitating.

"We will behave, be good, be seeing Michael," Fern said in one breath. "Surely will."

I didn't add my voice to my sisters' but I at least nodded. Then Pa said, "And Delphine will see to it that they do."

To him I said, "Yes, Papa."

"And it will be my treat," Pa's lady friend said.

There was screaming and cheering from Vonetta and

Fern. But Papa said, "Oh, no. Can't let you do that, Marva honey." And Vonetta and Fern had an "aw, shucks" fit.

"If you girls want to see these little boys sing and dance, you'll have to earn half the money for your tickets and refreshments," Pa said. "And I'll pay the other half."

I felt myself coming out of the sticky-honey sulk. If I knew anything, I knew how to earn my way.

Pa said, "If you pitch in around the house, you'll get a weekly allowance."

"I get a weekly allowance," I told Pa.

"They'll get one too," he said.

"But I work for mine," I said.

"They'll work for theirs too."

"Good idea," Miss Hendrix chirped. "That's a good idea, Lou." And then she reached over and kissed him, leaving her chicken oil and lipstick on his cheek.

"But you'll have to save your money," Pa said, ignoring the greasy kiss. "That means no chasing the ice-cream truck with every penny you earn," he said to Vonetta and Fern. "If you want my money, you'll have to save yours."

"Don't worry, Pa," I spoke up. "I'll make sure they save."

Then, at the part where Pa was supposed to pat me on the head for saying the right thing, Miss Marva Hendrix said, "Why can't Vonetta be in charge of saving?"

No one said a word. Hers was a shock of an idea that

caught anyone chewing or swallowing. Even Vonetta had to cough.

She got over the shock and said, "Yeah. Why can't I be in charge of the saving?"

"Because," I said, "the saver has to be responsible."

That should have fixed that, but nosy Miss Marva Hendrix said, "How will she learn responsibility if she's not given a chance?"

"I can learn responsibility," Vonetta chirped up. She looked worried.

"Surely can!" Fern added for solidarity.

Then Miss Hendrix asked, "What is with all this 'surely'?"

Later at the line for the bathroom, Vonetta and Fern went in together, leaving me alone with Miss Hendrix.

I said, "What if Vonetta loses the money we save?"

She stepped on my question right away with one of her own. "Delphine, do you know what a self-fulfilling prophecy is?"

I could have figured it out with more time than a second to answer but I said no. There was no point spinning straw and coming up all straw and no gold.

She said, "Don't wish for bad things to happen, Delphine. Vonetta deserves a chance."

I said, "I'm always in charge." I made sure I spoke Papa-calm and not Cecile-crazy, although I felt Cecile-crazy.

"Papa and Big Ma depend on me to look out for my sisters."

"I know you're older, Delphine, but if you keep your sisters down they'll never learn."

She might not have used the word, but I heard her calling me an oppressor. Someone who keeps the people down. It isn't oppression if you get whipped for what your sisters do and don't do. It's keeping them in line.

"I don't keep my sisters down," I said.

But she didn't say anything and neither could I. I was both angry and hurt. Nothing good could come out of my mouth. Certainly not gold.

Doves

We headed back to Herkimer Street after seeing Miss
Marva Hendrix off to her apartment in Brownsville. I let
Vonetta and Fern beat me out of the Wildcat and up the
steps so they could tell Big Ma all about our day with Pa's
lady friend. I would have felt a little giddy if Miss Marva
Hendrix hadn't soured the day by making me out to be
my sisters' oppressor.

I followed behind and unlocked the door while Vonetta
and Fern ran inside. I left the door cracked for Pa, who
was getting the blanket out of the trunk.

My sisters tried to clamor around Big Ma but she wanted
no part of them. She didn't want to hear about our outing with Miss Marva Hendrix, that we'd seen the Jackson

Five billboard, or that they were coming to New York City in December. She had a long, brownish-yellow envelope choked in her fist. And she looked confused while she turned left and then right like she was playing keep-away. I saw she'd been crying, so I said, "Vonetta. Fern. Quit it."

Big Ma threw herself in her chair and squeezed the envelope even more. "A mercy, Lord," Big Ma sobbed. "A mercy. A mercy."

Then Fern ran straight into me, ramming her head above my belly. She cried hard, almost biting me, while Vonetta went, "What's wrong? What's wrong?"

Then Pa walked in whistling, the blanket folded up in his arms. He saw Big Ma in the chair, put the blanket in my hands, and went to Big Ma. "Mama, Mama. What's the . . ." He saw the envelope and took it from her hands. "All right, Mama," he said calmly. "All right."

The envelope was still sealed, but crushed like Big Ma had been holding on to it for hours, waiting for us to come home. The hush over the house lay heavy, like snow sitting on our rooftop.

I felt bad news coming but I didn't want to hear it. Didn't want to hear it. And that was all I could fit in my prayer. That I didn't want to hear what the letter had to tell us.

Pa closed his eyes for a second. When he tore open the envelope, Big Ma cried out like he was tearing a part of her. Vonetta put her arms around Big Ma's neck while Big

Ma shuddered and cried. Before my eyes, Big Ma seemed to shrink inside her housedress.

"A mercy, a mercy. A mercy, Lord. A mercy."

To God, I said:

Don't let him be dead.

Don't let him be dead.

Don't let him be MIA. Or dead.

Then Pa said in his plain, warm voice, "Darnell's coming home." When he laid the envelope down on the stereo, I read the address in the corner: DEPARTMENT OF THE UNITED STATES ARMY. It had come special delivery and was addressed to THE FAMILY OF PFC DARNELL L. GAITHER. No wonder Big Ma had been afraid to open it.

Pa had to say it again: "Darnell's coming home, Ma." Finally she gasped for air, like a baby gasps before its first cry. Now Big Ma was all-out crying.

Fern unstuck her head from me and dried her face with my top.

After we'd gotten excited about the good news, Pa added, "He'll be in the hospital in Honolulu for two weeks. That's all." His voice sounded old, like when Cecile left us, and not light, like a man who whistled "My Girl."

I tried to ease myself back into normal breathing, but I imagined all the things that could have happened to him at war. Watching the soldiers and the people in Vietnam on the six o'clock news was the only time I was glad we didn't have color TV. They showed a lot on the news:

Dead soldiers. Prisoners of war. Wailing children, broken old people, bombing, and blood all came in sharp enough in black-and-white. The news anchor always said, "Parents, send the children out of the room if they're nearby." I was the only child in the room but I watched anyway.

Big Ma was now quietly sobbing, but Vonetta and Fern danced a hula because Pa had said "Honolulu" and I had to tell Heckle and Jeckle again to quit it.

"What happened to him?" I asked my father. "Did he get shot?"

"Shot by the enemy?" Vonetta added.

"Is Uncle Darnell almost dead?" Fern asked. "I thought he was dead."

Big Ma cried even more.

"Hush up," I told my sisters.

"You're not in charge. You can't hush nobody," Vonetta said.

"Surely can't."

"The two of you, hush up," Pa said.

Vonetta and Fern hushed.

Last year Mrs. Peterson asked our class if we were for the war or against it, or like the evening news anchor said, "hawks" or "doves." I said I was a hawk for my uncle Darnell and the soldiers he slept in foxholes and trampled through jungles with. But I didn't tell my class that I sometimes prayed at night that my uncle and the soldiers would kill the Vietcong who were trying to kill them. I didn't tell them how I prayed the same news anchor who told parents to shoo the kids out of the room would say, "Gather round, everybody. The war is over. The soldiers are all coming home."

But then they showed Vietnamese children shot up dead. And they showed bony Vietnamese people older than Big Ma, pointing to the sky and to the hills in the distance. Pointing to clouds of smoke and helicopters. They were never pointing at doves.

The Mummy Jar

Big Ma went to bed early that night. The US Army envelope coming and her thinking the worst about Uncle
Darnell had been too much. I remembered what Miss
Marva Hendrix had said. *Self-fulfilling prophecy.* I figured
she was saying that if you think something, it will happen.

Big Ma, Pa, Vonetta, Fern, and I had all thought the
worst, but now everything was all right. Uncle Darnell
would be home in two weeks. We would be under one
roof on Herkimer Street. Except for Cecile.

Later that evening, I stood by the entrance of the kitchen
after supper. "Where y'all going?" I asked Vonetta and

Fern. I folded my arms and tapped my foot to show I was serious.

"To brush our teeth," said one.

"And play Old Maid," said the other.

"You have a table to clear and dishes to wash and dry," I said.

"*You* have a table to clear and dishes to wash," one said.

"And dry," said the other.

"Oh yeah?" I asked.

"Oh yeah."

"Okay," I said calmly. "Then *you* can't be in charge of saving money if you don't have any money to save."

"We get an allowance," Vonetta said.

"Surely do," said the other. "Allowance."

"That's only if you do chores."

There was no comeback from the other side. I folded my arms and tapped my foot. Vonetta and Fern stood across from me and poked out their lips.

"You might be in charge of saving, but I'm in charge of giving out chores," I said. "And there's no allowance if I don't tell Papa you've earned it." I could have added, "So there," but my foot-tapping was good enough.

"What am I in charge of?" Fern asked.

"Everything else," I said.

I brought the serving platters and the Kool-Aid pitcher into the kitchen. Vonetta brought in the plates and made another trip for the glasses. Fern brought in the forks, spoons, and butter knife. I washed, Fern put the dishes in the rack, and Vonetta dried.

For everything we did, I put a check mark on a sheet I kept in my letter-writing pad.

When allowance day came, I found one dollar in quarters on my dresser next to my talcum powder. I kept two quarters for gum and Good & Plenty. Instead of putting the rest in my savings passbook, I gave Vonetta the other two quarters to put away for the concert.

Not to be outdone, Vonetta had made her own chart. *The Jackson Five at Madison Square Garden* was printed on top, all words spelled neatly and correctly. She had taken a ruler to make three columns and wrote our names at the top of each. She wrote *50¢* under my name, *5¢* under Fern's, and *10¢* under her own.

"I'm in charge of saving," Vonetta announced as if that was news. "So when you get allowance money and birthday money, you have to put it in the Madison Square Garden savings jar."

She sat an empty dill pickle jar on the table next to her savings chart. It made a nice, sharp knock against the table. She drew and colored a picture of five guys with Afros and glued that over the dill pickle label. The lid with its slot cut into the top was taped with many rounds of masking tape to the glass. It looked like a mummy jar instead of a savings jar.

"How'd you make that slot?" I asked, and ran my finger along its two-inch opening.

"She didn't slot it," Fern said. "Papa did it."

"Papa did that for you?"

"Yep," she said. "I taped the lid to the jar so no one can steal the money."

"Hope you washed out that jar real good with hot water and soap. Hope you washed away the dill-pickle smell."

"Smelly dill pickles!" Fern said. She found that to be funny.

"I'm the saver, Delphine. Stop trying to be in charge," Vonetta snapped. "I figured it out and we're doing it my way." She laid a sheet of paper next to her mummy jar. "You can't just drop money into the Jackson Five at Madison Square Garden savings jar."

"Surely can't."

"You have to deposit it like at the bank," she said. "The Jackson Five concert is in December. That's four months from now. So when Papa gives us our allowance, you write how much money you're putting in by your name next to 'week number one.' Every week I, the saver, add up what we put in. Then I minus that from the twelve dollars. That'll be our magic number. How much we'll need for the concert." Papa had promised to pay for the other half.

I couldn't believe she had thought up all of that. Vonetta

hated doing story problems in the third grade. She had even written *Take some of Fern's money* as her answer to a homework question about not having enough money to buy two bags of popcorn.

It nearly choked me to say it, but I did. "That's good, Vonetta."

"See, Delphine. You're not the only one good at being in charge."

I was only glad Miss Hendrix wasn't around to smile and say, "You see, Delphine. You were the oppressor. You tried to keep your sisters down."

Grade Six

I put on my new jumper. The one Lucy had shoved in Big Ma's hands. I felt ready for the sixth grade and couldn't wait to be in Miss Honeywell's class. She was the youngest, nicest teacher in the school and the best dresser. She assigned her class fun science, art, and history projects, and she wasn't a yeller like the other sixth-grade teachers.

I walked Fern down to where the second graders lined up. Vonetta broke away from us and ran off the minute she spotted her friends from last year. I didn't blame her. I couldn't wait to be away from my sisters and among my classmates. Although Frieda Banks lived a few blocks around the way from us, off Atlantic Avenue, we joined hands and swung them like we hadn't seen each other in ages. Then Lucy raced over, and so did Evelyn and Carmen and Monique and Rukia and the rest of the girls. The same old boys showed off trading cards and clowned around nearby. All except for Ellis Carter. Ellis was nowhere in sight, and I thought how lucky it would be if his family had moved to Queens or Staten Island.

I didn't care about the boys in my class but was so happy to be surrounded by the girls. Most of us were still eleven while some had already turned twelve. All of us wore hairstyles slightly different from our fifth-grade 'dos. Except for Rukia Marshall, a Malcolm X muslim whose hair was always covered by a scarf thing. Evelyn's and Monique's jumpers were like mine but in different colors. Lucy said it was about time I wore good clothes, but she didn't spill the beans that she had picked out my jumper two weeks ago. It was a sign that things were starting off right.

When the first bell rang, we formed two lines behind the cheese-gold "three" painted into the asphalt. Lucy, Frieda, and I couldn't wait to see what outfit Miss Honeywell wore and how she styled her hair. But instead of Miss Honeywell, a short, dark-skinned man stood facing our lines. "Classroom three," he said, "follow me, please."

We murmured as we followed him inside the building, up the steps to the sixth graders' floor, and into our new classroom. While we found seats, he wrote *Mr. Mwila* on the board, then pronounced it for us. *Mwee-lah* is how Miss Merriam Webster would have broken down his pronunciation. *Mwee-lah*. Although the letters of his name couldn't be said without showing teeth, I got the feeling he didn't mean to smile. Only to say his name.

"I am your new teacher," he said. "Welcome to grade six, classroom three."

There was some giggling because he didn't say it the right way—*welcome to the sixth grade, class six-three*—but also because he spoke with two accents. One was probably an African accent, and the other was like the queen of England's, but not like Ringo Starr's or Mick Jagger's.

Lucy spoke up for the rest of us. "Where's Miss Honeywell?"

"Didn't you hear?" Danny the K said. "She doing time, man."

"I'm not a man," Lucy said. "And she's not hardly in prison."

"Decorum, class," Mr. Mwila said sternly.

Of course no one knew what he'd just said, but the sharpness of his tone got our attention. He didn't answer Lucy's question, but instead said, "Now, class three. You have two minutes to find your seat for the school year. Once I call 'time,' your seat will be your permanent seat." He raised his watch, waited, and then said, "Class three, find your seats."

The class went crazy with chairs scraping and kids running, colliding, and laughing. Any boy who was on the right side of the classroom got up and ran to the left side. Any girl who sat on the left side ran to the right. Boys pushed their neighbors out of whatever desks they chose while Mr. Mwila looked on at the whole spectacle, nodding to himself. Rukia found out Monique wasn't her friend when Monique told her she couldn't sit there. That seat was for Carmen. Rukia took the desk nearest to the front that no one wanted. I was already on the girls' side of the room, so I stayed put. As long as Anthony, Ant, Danny the K, Enrique, the Jameses, the Michaels, Upton, and all of the other jokers were on the boys' side, I was fine. The desk to my left remained untaken, but with Lucy in front of me and Frieda at my right, I breathed easily. I was safe.

Outside of three new faces, not a whole lot had changed since Mrs. Peterson's class. It was as though someone had decided that we were family and couldn't be separated. The only difference was that the head of the classroom wasn't a woman in snappy, mod clothing but a short man in a dark suit who wasn't from Brooklyn.

Mr. Mwila raised his hand, his palm side showing and fingers spread wide. "Time."

It was at that moment that the classroom door opened and Ellis Carter walked in looking lost and happy and confused all at once. Lost after having wandered the hall. Happy to see his old boys from last year. Confused to see Mr. Mwila and not Miss Honeywell. His arms and legs seemed extra gangly and he loped around like he didn't know what to do with the extra inches he had grown.

"Do you belong in grade six, classroom three?"

Ellis shrugged, but Mr. Mwila didn't like that. "I don't understand this," Mr. Mwila said. He imitated Ellis's shrug, but sharper. "Either you belong in grade six, classroom three, or you belong elsewhere."

Ellis was a shrugger. He did it again. The boys laughed, thinking he was talking back, but with his body. "Here. I guess," Ellis said meekly enough to save him from walking the paddle mile to Principal Myers's office.

"Find a seat," Mr. Mwila said.

Ellis circled around long-legged and doofy. We all laughed through sealed lips to keep from laughing full out.

The only desks available were on the girls' side. Ellis probably thought if he circled around long enough, a seat would magically appear next to Danny the K or by one of the Jameses. He was out of luck on the boys' side, so he turned toward the desk all the way in the back of the class, behind Yvonne. Ellis Carter knew what was best for him. He didn't want to see the side of my face any more than I wanted to see the side of his squirrelly face from now until June. His jaw probably still stung every time he looked my way. He took a step to the back, but Mr. Mwila stopped him.

"Right here, young man," Mr. Mwila told him in a voice that said *Don't test me*. "The time for choice has passed.

96

You'll sit where I tell you to sit and you'll be on time for the start of class."

The boys broke out into, "Oh-ho, snaps!" Then Mr. Mwila shushed them without making a sound. Just a sharp eye and a finger to the lips.

"But . . . I don't want to sit with these . . . girls." Ellis looked like he was about to cry. He crunched himself down into the desk chair. One sneaker in each aisle.

Like it or not, I couldn't look to my left, in the direction of the teacher's desk, without seeing Ellis Carter.

The Subject Was Zambia

Usually the teacher played a name game on the first day of class, or she made name cards for our desks. Mr. Mwila placed a sheet on Rukia's desk. He told her to write her name in the first row, first column, then pass the sheet to the person behind her.

I waited for the sheet to reach my desk. There were only two male teachers in our entire elementary school, and none of us expected to have one until junior high school. I couldn't see why we needed a male teacher. Male teachers were for classrooms with rough and rowdy boys who needed a firm hand to keep them in line. The boys in our class were bigger pests than they were rough and rowdy. Last year Mrs. Peterson kept them in line easily with her pine "board of education." Mr. Mwila didn't carry a pine board. There was something about his voice that made the boys in our class straighten up and sit taller. Except for Ellis Carter. The sloucher.

He looked to Lucy and said, "Miss . . ."

"Lucy Raleigh," she said, happy to be called on.

He nodded. "Lucy Raleigh. You asked about Miss Honeywell. Now, I'll answer. Have you heard of exchange students?"

"Yes," Lucy answered. "When a student from here, the US, switches places with a student from another country."

Mr. Mwila clapped his hands once. "I couldn't have said it better."

Lucy blew on her nails and dusted her collar.

"Your Miss Honeywell and I have switched places," he said. "We're exchange teachers. She's in my country, Zambia, and I'm here with you."

Sounds of amazement spread across the room. Miss Honeywell was in Zambia, sharing her fun projects with students who didn't know how lucky they were. It wasn't fair.

"It is only for a year," he said. "I'm excited about this opportunity, but I'll be glad to see my wife and children this time next year." Then Mr. Mwila finally gave us a real smile as if he was embarrassed or had said more than he meant to.

He crossed to the center of the room and pulled the

map of the world down over the blackboard. He grabbed the long, wooden pointer from the chalk ledge and aimed it at an area that looked like a bitten-into golden pear, near the middle, southern part of Africa. "This is my country. Zambia.

"Four years ago at the Olympics, our athletes went to France as Northern Rhodesians while a revolution was under way in our country. By the end of the Olympic Games, those same athletes left the stadium with a new flag and a new name: Zambia."

He said *revolution* on the first day of class, just like Sister Mukumbu had taught us about revolution and spinning and changing on our first day at the People's Center. But he didn't ask us if we knew the meaning of *revolution*, so I couldn't raise my hand and define it for the class. It was as if he expected us to know the meaning, along with the other words he used, like *decorum*.

Instead of asking us how we spent our summer, he told us more about his country. He answered questions about mining, and silly Tarzan questions about witch doctors and wild animals. While things were going well, he said, "Now class, suppose Zambia was the main subject of a report. . . ."

We all groaned. Our new teacher expected us to think about writing reports while Miss Honeywell's new class was making papier-mâché volcanoes with bicarbonate lava.

"What could some of the minor topics of our report be? I will give you a hint. I spoke of at least five subtopics. Who can name a subtopic?"

Mr. Mwila's eyes shone brightly at us. He expected twenty-four hands to shoot up, but not one hand rose. Not even Rukia's or Michael Sandler's. We thought we were learning about the place where Miss Honeywell was, not preparing to write a report on a country we hadn't heard of before Mr. Mwila brought us up to our classroom. The room went silent.

"Come, come, grade six," Mr. Mwila said. "You know these subtopics. Jump in. Name one."

Rukia raised her hand. Mr. Mwila glanced down at his classroom sheet and said, "Rukia." He said it with the same teeth-baring smile he used to say his own name.

"Can one of the subjects be the early settlers in Zambia?"

"Indeed it can," Mr. Mwila said. "Early settlers in Zambia. Who else will we hear from?" He searched the room for another raised hand, but everyone kept their hands down, and Rukia knew better than to raise hers again.

"Ah!" he said. He pulled the map back up, took a piece of chalk, and made two horizontal lines on the board. A vertical line went under the horizontal line on the right side of the board. "Girls' team, one point."

I knew what he was doing. The Black Panthers warned us about this in summer camp. Divide and conquer.

Separate the people and make one side think they are different or better than the other.

But girls *were* better than boys.

Mr. Mwila's plan worked. Hands shot up on the boys' side, starting with the Jameses, Enrique, Anthony but not Ant, Upton, and Michael Sandler, the smartest of the three Michaels. Then Ellis Carter raised his hand to show boy-team solidarity although he sat on our side. It was a wonder Mrs. Peterson had promoted him to the sixth grade with the rest of us. Ellis did his homework and passed his quizzes fine. But call on him to speak and you could barely hear his voice. Except when he sang that stupid dolphin song at me. I put an end to that dolphin singing.

"Ellis Carter."

Ellis, who was caramel red to begin with, got a little redder. He stamped his foot.

"Come, come. The boys have yet to score a point."

Ellis mumbled, "I lost my . . . lost my . . . forgot my . . . what I was going to say."

"Girls," Mr. Mwila said.

The chorus of Jameses, Michaels, Anthonys, and the rest told Ellis he stunk now that he was a girl.

"What about our turn?" Michael Sandler asked Mr. Mwila.

"Your representative has spoken," Mr. Mwila said. "In your football terms, he punted."

We girls didn't really know football terms—American or any other kind—but we understood our teacher. Then all of us girls raised our hands. My subject was going to be political change and revolution. I couldn't wait to say exactly that.

"Frieda," Mr. Mwila said.

"Is another subject foot—" She stopped in the middle of her thought. "Is another subject the national pastimes in Zambia?" After all, Mr. Mwila spoke of more activities than football, and Frieda must have figured out how a list of activities made one subject.

Mr. Mwila made another tally under "girls" and we began to cheer. Ellis put his head down on his desk.

"Boys," Mr. Mwila said, "there is still an opportunity for redemption."

The boys shouted, "Redemption!" when I knew half of them didn't know what *redemption* meant.

"If you correctly supply another subtopic, you'll be rewarded with a bonus point and you'll be equal to the girls."

The girls' team called out that it was unfair to give the boys a bonus point. Mr. Mwila only said, "Decorum," and the boys laughed.

"Who will take up the call for the dignity and redemption of the boys?"

The girls booed but the boys waved their arms like flags. Then Michael Sandler called out to his side like a football coach, "Only if you know the answer," and half of the boys lowered their flags.

"Well then," Mr. Mwila said, "perhaps you'd like to supply another subject for the point and the bonus point. You are . . . Michael Sandler."

"That's my name," Michael said.

"Mr. Michael Sandler," Mr. Mwila said. Lucy grinned.

Michael cleared his throat. "A subtopic to a report about Zambia is: What are the chief exports of Zambia?" His answer sounded so right, and he said it like Huey Newton addressing the masses. The boys cheered. Mr. Mwila raised his hands and we immediately got quiet.

Lucy turned to me and winked. Didn't she know that Michael S. liked Evelyn Alvarez?

"Michael Sandler," he said, "I didn't say 'export' and yet you used the right term. You have earned the point and the bonus, and the boys are now equal to the girls."

The boys cheered, but Michael Sandler didn't join in because he caught Mr. Mwila's joke.

But then the joke was on us. We spent the next period writing paragraphs about Zambia, choosing one minor subject.

I didn't want to be the class goody but I couldn't help myself. At the end of our first day I told Mr. Mwila, "My mother's name is from Africa."

He smiled and said, "Miss . . ." He didn't have his name

sheet and hadn't learned my name.

"Delphine. Delphine Gaither."

"Yes, yes. Delphine." Another smile. His eyes were kind. "What country is your mother from?"

I was a little confused but answered, "America."

"I see," Mr. Mwila said, although I wasn't sure what he could see.

I couldn't remember the country she'd said her name was from but I knew it was the land of our ancestors. I knew it sounded like Aruba but I didn't think that was right.

I gave the only answer I could give with certainty. "Her name is Nzila." And when I said it I smiled without meaning to.

"Ah!" said Mr. Mwila, recognizing the name instantly. "Your mother was born on the road. It must be a fascinating story."

I looked at him strangely. I didn't know what to say.

"The hospital is far if you live on the outskirts, so many children are born on the way. Nzila's also popular if your parents travel. Some stories about the name are funnier than others."

I was still stunned and asked, "Doesn't it mean blowing away the dust from the surface, or something about truth?"

Mr. Mwila said, "Is that what your mother said?"

There I was nodding, because I couldn't speak. That

was what I deserved for throwing myself and my mother on display like Vonetta would. All it got me was a mother who lied about what her stupid poet name meant. Big Ma and Pa were right to keep Cecile from naming Fern any ooga-mooga names.

Dear Cecile,

>*How are you?*
>*I am not fine.*
>*My new teacher is Mr. Mwila from Zambia in southern Africa. Mr. Mwila told me the truth about Nzila when I told him your African name. He said Nzila means born on the road. It does not come from Aruba, the land of our ancestors. It comes from Zambia. It has nothing to do with the truth.*
>*It isn't fair to tell us your name means blowing the dust off of surfaces when it means born on the road.*
>*At least I know better.*

Sincerely,
Delphine

YOUR MotheR. Nzila

It took no time at all for me to turn against my mother when I had scolded Vonetta and Fern for wanting to be flower girls at Pa's wedding to another woman.

My letter yelled at my mother. It said she didn't tell us the truth about her name. That was the same as calling my own mother a liar.

I thought Cecile would send a letter to Vonetta, one to Fern, and no letter to me. The next week her letter came addressed to me. Airmail.

Dear Delphine,

I am a human being. A black human being. A female.

A woman. A poet. That is the order I came into the world. I see as only I can see things. As only a poet would see things.

Words do more, mean more, than how they are defined. I see things visible, invisible, ordinary, and extraordinary in the world.

If a child born on the road is named Nzila, then I can call myself that.

If that child grows into a girl who sleeps out in the street, then that is who I am. My name is growing up with me. As I am defined, then my name is defined and shaped around me like clothing.

If that woman finds her road hard, but full of meaning that she makes sense of and sees clearly through lines of poetry, then she can say she has found truth. She blows dust off the surface of a clouded path. She can call herself that.

One day you'll see the truth in things. Until then, study hard.

Your Mother.
Nzila

P.S. You are not grown. Be who you are. Eleven.

⭐ Hooah

A few weeks sped by, but the leaves on the trees were still green. No one was happier than Big Ma that time was moving along. You'd think she'd be singing a song and doing the Charleston, but happiness didn't stop Big Ma from picking a fuss with Pa. I wasn't supposed to hear what Big Ma said to Papa that morning, but I did. In spite of Big Ma saying "Welcome to the family" to Miss Hendrix, my grandmother put her foot down about Miss Hendrix coming along with us. "There's only room for family," she told Pa. "It's only right."

It didn't take much to put together what I overheard. Papa wanted Miss Hendrix to come with us to bring Uncle Darnell home from Fort Hamilton, but Big Ma was against it. Even though we'd be driving down Fourth Avenue through Bay Ridge in the car Pa paid for, Big Ma got her way. Before we left, Pa called Miss Hendrix and spoke really low on the phone in the kitchen.

It's strange to remember that your grown father is someone else's child. Even in the house he built up nearly from scratch, he was still Big Ma's child. Though he often made like he didn't hear her, he did mind her. With most things. Not everything. He sent us out to Oakland to get to know our mother, even when Big Ma spoke against it every day until we went, and every other day after we returned. That time, it didn't matter what Big Ma said. Pa had made up his mind and we flew to Oakland to get to know our mother.

That day Big Ma won. Or Pa let her win. I didn't want Miss Marva Hendrix to come with us, but I didn't want anyone to be over my father. Not even his mother.

We'd been to Fort Hamilton once before. We came last year to wave good-bye to Uncle Darnell as he stood along with the other soldiers, most of them probably like him—fresh out of high school. It was easy to lose sight of him, but I could pick out my uncle among the rows of soldiers in those sad green uniforms. His ugly green army bag lifted on his back along with a rifle. When the soldiers marched and made a sharp left turn, I saw that hat sitting on top of my uncle's shaven head. I was filled with the last feeling I expected. Pride.

All of us except for Fern waved furiously as the trumpets, trombones, tubas, flutes, and percussion instruments played the marching tune. The booming drums and clashing cymbals frightened Fern, and she clung to me. But each time the drums boomed and the cymbals clashed, the soldiers marched harder and seemed taller. Like those thundering drums, their hearts were booming through their sad green uniforms. They marched straight ahead and made crisp turns without looking over to family members, girlfriends, and even a high school football team that had come in team jackets to wave them off. The brass horns and booming drums marched the soldiers onto army trucks covered in the same green material as their uniforms and army bags. Then the trucks drove away while we waved and Fern and Big Ma cried.

It was now a year and two months later. Pa showed the soldier at the guardhouse his driver's license and asked for the "discharge site." The soldier wore a black MP band around his arm, "MP" for military police. He tried to meet Pa with eagle eyes, but he seemed young. Much younger than Pa's thirty-two years. I wondered if he had ever aimed his rifle and stared down a flower girl eagle-eyed at a protest rally when he really wanted to dance with her at the senior prom.

He directed Pa where to go, and Pa gave him a sharp nod.

We drove by redbrick buildings and white buildings, an army tank with a big white star painted on it, and long, iron cannons. They were old cannons from old wars, now just army decorations.

Pa parked the Wildcat and we walked toward the field of grass the young MP had pointed out. Fern held Pa's hand while Big Ma, Vonetta, and I lagged behind without talking. Big Ma was talking silently. Just not to us. She was filled up with prayer and had been talking to the Lord all morning. She had only broken prayer to fuss with Pa about Miss Marva Hendrix.

At least the grass was a pretty green.

When we made it across the field, the soldiers were already standing in lines. Some used crutches, and I counted at least five soldiers in wheelchairs. I thought all of the soldiers were men until I made out a line of women in those green army uniforms and boots. When I asked Pa, he said they were probably nurses.

Not long after we were seated, the ceremony got started. The band played "The Star Spangled Banner." We stood and said the Pledge of Allegiance as if we were in class. The army chaplain said a few words and a councilman from the mayor's office thanked the soldiers for their service. A soldier, probably a leader or sergeant, gave what sounded like three deep chest coughs, and at each cough the soldiers moved. Then he said, "Company: discharged," and some of the soldiers shouted a big "Hooah!"

or yelled, and some said nothing. The band played, and even though there were more fifes, clarinets, and flutes than booms and brass, Fern held on to Pa tighter.

I knew Uncle Darnell's head from all the rest. Even though he didn't have to kneel, Uncle Darnell got down on one knee and held out his arms. Fern forgot how scared she was and went running to him and jumped up into Uncle Darnell's arms. It was the first time I saw that Fern was getting too big to be jumping in someone's arms. Vonetta only saw that she wasn't being hugged and said, "What about me?" tapping her toe. Uncle Darnell said, "Get over here, Net-Net. Sugar me up." Uncle Darnell had been saying that to us for as long as I could remember. It was funny because his skin tasted of salt when my lips finally reached his cheek.

I was so glad to see my uncle and to just have him here. Here, right here. Standing before us with everything he went overseas with. Arms and legs. No bandages or crutches.

Big Ma could walk perfectly well, but she moved like she was hurt, and Pa had to help her along. When she reached Uncle Darnell, he stood up and wrapped himself around her or she wrapped herself around him and they didn't let go for a long, long time.

He and Pa embraced, but only for a few seconds. Then Pa slapped Darnell on the back and they shook hands.

He took off his hat and put it on Vonetta's head, and

boy, did she like that. She said, "Uncle Darnell, I'm bringing you to school for show-and-tell."

Then Big Ma said, "Oh, no, you're not. Take that army hat for show-and-tell and be glad you have that. And that your uncle is home." Then Big Ma started to cry again. I could have kicked Vonetta.

Pa was about to grab his green army bag but Uncle Darnell reached and got it, as if Pa was too old and too weak.

When we all walked across the field toward the Wildcat, I kept looking at us. All of us. I couldn't help but see how much Uncle Darnell looked like Pa and Big Ma. Then, how we looked like him. And how we looked like Pa and Cecile. And Big Ma. How we all fit together even though Cecile was thousands of miles away. But I knew Cecile and Pa didn't fit together. And she and Big Ma never fit together. But at least I could see how my sisters and I were both Gaithers and Johnsons. And that was just fine. For now, walking with my family, I felt good and selfish, which was how Cecile told me to be, one night in Oakland. I enjoyed having my uncle, my father, my grandmother, and my sisters all to myself. I enjoyed the way it used to be in our house on Herkimer Street.

Uncle D's Bag

Uncle Darnell had things he didn't have when he left for boot camp and then Vietnam—and I'm not talking about things in his duffel bag. He had a harder, older look on his face, like he'd never do the Watusi again. I could see it in his eyes the same way I could see Big Ma filling up with prayer even when she wasn't saying a word. Uncle D was darker. Probably from being out in the sun. His brows sat atop his eyes, protecting them like he still needed shade. Veins I'd never noticed before streamed along his arms and legs. He had hard and sharp muscles where he was lean and smooth. I didn't know how the jungle smelled, but whenever I hugged him I smelled wild tree vines beneath his shaving cream and toothpaste. One thing was for sure. He had given Pa all of his dimples, and Pa had given Uncle Darnell his long face.

We tried to give our uncle breathing room but we hung on to him every minute of the day. Even when we weren't on him physically, we surrounded him. We just couldn't stop, and as he tried to put himself in order we gathered around him, excited like puppies, waiting for him to pull exciting things out of that tall green bag.

"Delphine has a boyfriend," Fern tattled.

"Is that so?" My uncle looked straight at me and I felt my skin warming up.

"He's my pen pal," I said, trying not to make a big deal of it. If I put up a fuss my sisters would never stop teasing me.

"But he doesn't write her any letters so she has to dream about him," Vonetta added.

"I do not dream about him."

Heckle and Jeckle performed up a storm for Uncle Darnell. Heckle became Hirohito writing letters about love and go-karts, and Jeckle became me and wrote back in letters about love and Jackie Jackson. Uncle Darnell gave them the little bit of haw-hawing they were after and then told them to cut it out.

"Tanya Bailey," Vonetta said, "got silk pajamas when her daddy came home from Vietnam."

"Who'd want some old silk pajamas?" Uncle Darnell asked, his eyes twinkling.

"We would!" we said all at once.

"Is that so?" he asked.

"Yeah, Unc. We want a souvenir," I said, glad that the subject had changed.

"So cough it up," Vonetta said.

"Start coughing, Uncle Darnell," Fern said.

"Only thing I got in here are dirty socks, dirty drawers, a helmet, and a canteen," he said.

"Y'all leave your uncle alone," Big Ma scolded. "He just got home and you're on him like he's Santa Claus. Let him rest."

We still sat around him, waiting to see what would come out of his bag. To our disappointment, he pulled out a canteen, a helmet, and a lot of army things. Then he grinned like my old uncle, and he didn't look hardened and long-faced like I had thought. He hummed and grinned like he had that time he braided Vonetta's and Fern's hair together, and they couldn't get unloosened from each other. He dragged out the suspense, poking around at the bottom of his bag until we yelled, "Uncle D!" Then he pulled out some folded cloth. Silk cloth. Two blue. One yellow. When he threw them to us, each cloth opened to silk robes and we screamed and paraded around in them. Vonetta was hard to live with. She got the yellow silk robe.

Big Ma outdid herself cooking up all of Uncle Darnell's favorites. He sat and talked more than he ate, and Big Ma kept clucking and fussing. "What's the matter, son? Don't you like your chicken-fried steak? Only he and Pa had those huge cuts of floured and fried meat on their plates. Vonetta, Fern, Big Ma, and I had make-believe steaks. Pork chops.

Uncle Darnell left a lot of food on his plate. Before I could get a piece of his steak, Big Ma slapped my hand, grabbed his plate, and wrapped it in tinfoil. "I'll heat it up when you're hungry." She shook her head. "Those Vietcong took my baby's stomach. At least you're home, praise the Lord."

"Praise the Lord," we all sang, including Pa. We meant it in a joking way. Big Ma wasn't pleased.

Pa and Uncle Darnell stayed up talking, then the house fell quiet and every light in our house went out.

I was in a deep, happy sleep. I soon awoke to banging and shouting. Then heavy footsteps that ran from Pa's bedroom into the parlor room where Uncle Darnell slept. I heard Pa's and Big Ma's voices.

"Easy, man. Take it easy."

"A mercy, Jesus. A mercy."

And "You're home, man. Look around, Darnell. You're home."

Fern came running out of her room but Big Ma told her to get on back to bed. She came running into my room and jumped into my bed.

"Delphine. They're shooting Uncle D."

"No one's shooting at Uncle D."

"Vietnam's shooting him." She said "Be at nam."

"Vietnam's way over there, Fern," I told her. "Uncle had a bad dream."

"He's scared, Delphine. Uncle D's scared." And she looked scared.

"He'll go back to sleep," I told her. "He'll be okay."

Half-moons and Squiggles

Mr. Mwila walked down the space that separated the girls and Ellis Carter from the boys, to hand out our second attempt at essay writing. I twisted and craned to catch an Excellent, Very Good, Good, or Satisfactory on someone's paper. I couldn't help but be competitive. If Ellis got a Very Good, I knew I'd get an Excellent. If Frieda earned an Excellent, I knew I'd get a Very Good. But if Frieda got a Very Good, I'd have to be content with Good. Even after a few weeks I didn't know what kind of marker Mr. Mwila was. He explained things, brought in articles for social studies, and demonstrated how things worked in science and in math more than he quizzed us, so it was hard to know if I'd be skipping along or struggling like on heavy laundry days.

No one with an essay in their hand was saying anything, but they studied their marked sheets and made faces before turning their papers right-side down.

Lucy received her paper and did a little chair dance. I wrote better than Lucy, so I grew cheerfully anxious to get my paper.

While I had been watching my classmates, Mr. Mwila had placed my essay on my desk swiftly and then gave Ellis his paper.

Finally. I saw what everyone else had seen. Red squiggles. Lines. Dots. Horizontal half-moons jumped from one word over others to get to another word. The words beneath the horizontal half-moons had a line running through them that ended in a squiggle. The poor words looked like a wriggling trout on a speared hook. I also found myself making faces at my own paper. And then I got to the end of the page where the only words written were: *Good first effort. See me.*

I leaned to quickly read Ellis's paper. *Good first effort.* Then I turned to my right to see Frieda's paper. Her paper also had a lot of the same squiggles, half-moons, and the words *Good first effort.* No matter which way I turned my neck, no one else had *See me* following their *Good first effort.*

I pushed my fat pink eraser over the *See me* and tried to look up at the board like nothing was wrong, but my stomach quaked. I couldn't imagine why Mr. Mwila wanted to see me. With all of those red lines and squiggles dancing around on my essay, I wasn't foolish enough to think he meant to tell me anything good. If Mr. Mwila had anything wonderful to tell me, he would have used a gold star or written *Excellent* across my paper.

"According to Miss Merriam Webster, solidarity means being of one mind." I couldn't have thought of a better way to begin my essay. Solidarity was my main subject. From there I wrote how the Black Panthers used "solidarity" to talk about "the people" being united as one people. I couldn't figure out why my teacher wanted to see me.

Danny the K raised his hand and before he was called on, he said, "What does all this mean, Mr. Mwila?" He was echoed by yeahs, one of them mine.

Mr. Mwila said, "You have submitted your first drafts to me and I have returned them."

"Giraffe!" Danny the K said. "Did Mr. Mwila say 'giraffe'?"

"Daniel McClaren." Mr. Mwila was firm but calm. "The corner."

Danny the K stood up without protest and slinked to the front of the room. He stood facing the corner with his hands by his sides.

"Now," Mr. Mwila said, "you've written your first drafts."

He wrote the word on the blackboard. *Draft.*

When Big Ma said "draft" she spoke about our cold house during the winter. When Uncle Darnell said "draft" he meant he was going into the army to fight the war. I knew our teacher wasn't talking about a cold house or the army. Still, it was a wonder Miss Merriam Webster kept everything straight in her dictionary.

Mr. Mwila told us everything about what a first draft is and what a great opportunity a first draft provides. He said a first draft isn't meant to be marked on, because it was an "idea paper." First drafts are meant to be thought about. Rethought. Then rewritten. And wasn't it good to have a chance to improve upon our first effort?

He didn't mean for us to answer, but we all said no. Even Rukia.

I was certain no other sixth-grade class was being taught how to write an essay this way. Main subjects. Subtopics. First drafts. Second drafts. Squiggles and half-moons. And no grades.

Mr. Mwila thought his teaching was just grand. He drew each squiggle and explained what it meant. "Proof-reading marks and drafts go hand in hand."

"Like Michael Sandler and Evelyn Alvarez," someone piped up from the boys' side when Mr. Mwila was turned toward the board.

Evelyn tossed her head to deny that she was Michael's girlfriend. It wasn't official, but Evelyn's brothers let

Michael walk to school with them, and they weren't friends with him. Everyone knew he was really walking with Evelyn. At least Evelyn didn't have to worry if anyone would ask her to the sixth-grade dance.

That didn't stop Lucy from liking Michael Sandler.

When the second bell rang, the students with musical instruments went to band class and the rest of us were on our way to chorus. Before I reached the door, Mr. Mwila stopped me. I had forgotten about the *See me* but he hadn't. Lucy and Frieda waited for me but he told them to hurry along to class.

I stood at his desk not knowing what to expect.

"Delphine," he said. "You're in grade six?"

I nodded and couldn't figure out why he started out asking what he already knew.

"As such, you're a leader in this school. An upperclasswoman. You're in the highest grade in our school."

And taller than every boy, except Ellis, and taller than most teachers. Including Mr. Mwila.

I answered, "Yes," to break myself from nodding.

"Then how is it that an upperclasswoman in grade six would believe Merriam-Webster was female?"

I heard his question correctly. His accents were so clear. The King's English and whatever his people spoke in Zambia. I heard him but I was in shock like I had

124

walked into a glass wall. I didn't know what to say. He had to repeat the thing he had just told me. "How is it that an upperclasswoman in grade six would believe Merriam-Webster was a female?"

"She is," I told him. "Isn't she?" My breathing was fast and my mouth dry.

"Delphine Gaither. I'm excusing you from chorus this period. Instead, you'll go to the library and write an essay on Merriam-Webster. So, first, you'll go to the encyclopedia for an overview. Then seek out other sources and begin your essay."

"Sources?"

"Books. Magazines articles that you'll use in your essay."

Mr. Mwila must have seen my eyes filling up. He scribbled a pass quickly so I wouldn't be standing there crying in front of him. "Go now."

Lucy and Frieda were waiting for me in the hall. I wished they had gone on to chorus. They could see my face. Tears about to roll. I sniffed back the snot and blinked back the tears.

"Delphine, you're in trouble?" Lucy asked. "Did you write some Black Panther stuff? Girl, you can't write that stuff in school."

"She can write Black Power papers," Frieda said. Her brother was in the Brooklyn chapter. "John-Isaac will have an army of Brooklyn Panthers down here if you want."

I wanted to cry and was still in shock, not knowing what to tell my friends. Then Mr. Mwila said it for me: "Lucy Raleigh. Frieda Banks. To chorus. Now."

They shot me looks of sympathy and solidarity before taking off. I walked to the library and showed the librarian my note.

I did as Mr. Mwila told me. I went straight to the reference section and found the Encyclopedia Britannicas. I took the *M* for *Merriam* and the *W* for *Webster*, just in case, and brought the heavy, leather-bound books over to a table. I dried my eyes some more and started with the search for Merriam. But I didn't find her. Instead, it was as Mr. Mwila had said. She turned out to be a he. And he was three he's. There was a Noah Webster and two Merriam brothers. My eyes flooded up before I could read any of it. And then I just put my head down and cried. There were other kids in the library but I couldn't stop crying.

I felt the way Fern must have felt when she found her doll baby, Miss Patty Cake, all blacked-up thanks to Vonetta's Magic Marker. Like someone she loved had been turned into a joke and taken away from her.

I'd had a picture of Miss Merriam Webster in my head for so long. I heard her showing me where to look for words. How to pronounce them. What they meant. How to spell them. I imagined she was plain, and that it was all right to be plain.

When I finished crying, I knew I had to do like Fern

had done with Miss Patty Cake. I had to leave Miss Merriam Webster and all my pictures of her behind.

I asked Mr. Mwila if I could just do my paper over, and he nodded.

Brooklyn Magic

Uncle Darnell had been home for a few weeks, but he still woke up in the middle of the night. I'd hear the floorboards creak under his footsteps but I'd pretend to be asleep. From my window I'd watch him leave out the front door and walk down Herkimer Street. Pa told Big Ma Uncle D spent a lot of time in Fulton Park with the other soldiers who were home from Vietnam. Then I wouldn't see him until we came in from school and he'd be laid out on his bed in the parlor room where Cecile slept when my father and uncle first took her in.

We got home from school and found Uncle Darnell buttoning his shirt, getting ready to go out. He said he was going to the candy store around the corner and we asked if we could go with him. He said, "Drop your books and come on." Uncle Darnell was always easy that way.

"Put on your army clothes," Vonetta said. "So we can show everybody."

Uncle Darnell almost grinned, but he didn't give his all-out dimpled grin. "Show 'em what, Net-Net?"

Without missing a beat Vonetta said, "That you been to Vietnam."

Fern added, "Fighting the war."

He made a low hum. "They know," he said. "'Sides. Better to show 'em I'm back home, right?"

"Right on," Vonetta said. Then Fern had to say it too.

Uncle Darnell wore what he called his "civvies." His regular clothes. We were so glad to have him home and just walk with him. We also knew he'd buy us candy or take us down to the record shop so we could moon over the Jackson Five album. We'd be with our uncle, moon over the Jackson Five, and get candy without spending money that could go toward our Madison Square Garden savings.

We passed by Friendship Baptist without Uncle Darnell making mention of the Arabian Knight or his sword, plastered into the yellow brick face of the church. The pastor said the church had been built by an Arabian Order of Shriners decades before Friendship Baptist made it its spiritual home. Uncle Darnell used to tell us stories about the Arabian Knight and how he died defending this block from urban decay and that his face had been immortalized in plaster to keep watch over Herkimer Street. Vonetta, Fern, and I were so giddy about candy and maybe strolling over to the record shop that we hadn't noticed that our uncle didn't say what he always said when we walked by the Arabian Knight: "He's got his mystic eye on us."

Instead, we called out to anyone on their stoop or in the street, "Our uncle is back from Vietnam." Mrs. Allen from Friendship Baptist was the first person we called out to. She said, "Bet you're glad you don't have to go back."

Uncle Darnell said, "Don't you know it." He sounded old, like Pa. Not young like someone out of high school for a year and three months. The men mostly shook his hand and thanked him for doing his duty. But one man said, "I wouldn't go to no foreign country and shoot up poor people." Vonetta got mad and said, "My uncle did not go to Vietnam and shoot up poor people." Fern said, "He shot the enemy." I didn't say anything. I listened to what the newscasters said about the soldiers harming civilians and doing worse. But I also knew my uncle didn't do any of those things while he was in Vietnam. I just couldn't open my mouth.

"Come on, y'all," Uncle Darnell told us. "Peace, man," he said to the guy who wouldn't even look at him. *Peace, man.*

* * *

One day when he was in Vietnam, I'd gotten a letter from
him that said:

Delphine,

Everything's all right.
Everything's out of sight.

Love you love you
Uncle D

His crazy, loopy handwriting swam around that yellow,
lined paper. I showed the letter to Pa and Big Ma.

Pa said, "That boy's trying to sing you a Stevie Wonder
tune in a letter." And he laughed a big, whopping laugh,
which Papa didn't hardly do.

I figured Pa was right. Uncle D was writing me a letter
and hearing a familiar song in his mind. Maybe the bombing and shooting had started and he had to write fast.
That was why his writing was nothing like the writing on
his other letters. Uncle Darnell made his letters tall and
lean slightly to the right, like I did. Then I remembered.
He taught me how to handwrite the alphabet before I
went to school.

* * *

The air was a little crisp, and Uncle Darnell's nose started to run, so he wiped it on his sleeve. He had written to me about how it rained off and on in Vietnam, but Vietnam rain couldn't top Brooklyn chill in early October. Uncle D never mentioned getting sick over there, but now he always kept a cold.

We stepped out into Bedford Avenue, and Fern, who hadn't forgotten, looked up at the armory and cried, "Say it, Uncle Darnell. Say it!" She might have walked past the Arabian Knight but she hadn't forgotten about the princess.

He looked around like he was lost in thought. Then he came back to us and said, "Huh?" like he didn't remember we were on the corner and could see the armory and how its round towers rose into the sky like the Magic Kingdom. It was the storybook place at Bedford and Atlantic, where the princess had been calling out to be rescued since Fern was about four or five.

When he said, "Huh?" Fern started it off to help him remember. "Who will save the princess locked in the red castle?"

Vonetta said, "That's for babies, baby."

Fern said, "Take that back, Vonetta."

The sun was in Uncle Darnell's eyes. He blinked a few times. "I forgot how it went," he said.

"You say, 'I hear a voice,' then I say, 'The princess is

crying. The princess is crying.' Then you say, 'Who will save the princess in the red castle?' Then I say, 'We will save the princess in the red castle.' Then we charge to her rescue."

"Right, right," Uncle said, but I doubted he really remembered. Or maybe his mind was somewhere else.

Sonny Bono Has a Big Nose

Mr. Mwila told Anthony to close the blinds while he flipped the light switch to make the room dark. There is something about sudden darkness in a classroom of twenty-four sixth graders that sets off mischief. There was giggling on one side of the room. Spitballs on the other. Then Mr. Mwila flipped the light switch on and said, "Anthony." Anthony and Ant looked up, one guiltier than the other, although Mr. Mwila had clearly spoken to Anthony this time and not Antnee.

"I didn't do it!" Anthony cried.

"I didn't accuse," Mr. Mwila said, as cool as Sidney Poitier telling off the white racist sheriff in the movie *In the Heat of the Night*. He pulled the plug out of the wall socket and carefully wound the cord in circles. "Anthony," he began again, "please open the blinds."

Anthony got up and drew the blinds open.

"Upton," Mr. Mwila said, "please wheel the projector to the audiovisual room." We felt his cool, but we also felt his anger underneath. We were in trouble.

"Grade six, classroom six-three . . ."

Big trouble, I thought. He had called us by our formal name, like when your mother or grandmother calls you by all of your names to keep from calling you something worse.

"Take out your math notebooks. We shall have double period math."

Mr. Mwila didn't raise his voice or take out the "pine board of education" like Mrs. Peterson had done time and time again. Instead, "Sidney Poitier" said, "You can't behave as you did in the fifth grade. When you behave like the upperclassmen and upperclasswomen that you are, we'll engage in grade-six activities. Now, notebooks on desks."

I had yet to make a really good, face-to-face impression on my teacher, and now he was disappointed with us all. I didn't want Mr. Mwila to catch me giggling or going, "Aw, shucks," over having to do two periods of math.

Michael S. raised his hand and was recognized. "Mr. Mwila," he said—and Lucy practically swooned—"it isn't fair. Why should we all be punished because someone"—he looked at Ant—"threw the first spitball?"

"This isn't a punishment, Michael. It's an opportunity. If we can't conduct ourselves with decorum during the film, we'll jump ahead with mathematics, and what can be better than to leap ahead?" He smiled at us as though he had offered us something wonderful. "Homework tonight will be that much easier after this extra time."

The next day after lunch, the film projector stood on its cart in the back of the room. Mr. Mwila said, "We shall try again."

Shall was a storybook word that Uncle Darnell never used in bedtime stories of Arabian Knights or princesses locked in the tower. *Shall* was in one of our school assembly songs, "We Shall Overcome." But only Mr. Mwila used *shall* for everyday talking. And now that I'd grown used to his voice, I couldn't imagine him not saying *shall* or *decorum*.

Mr. Mwila made the room as dark as it could get and turned on the projector. No one wanted to "leap ahead" with more decimals, so the room was quiet.

Since separate health classes were no longer taught at our school, each sixth-grade class had to watch six health-and-safety films. Then in the spring, the sixth-grade girls watched a seventh film while the boys got an extra period of gym. The school figured our mothers could tell us everything we needed to know about the five basic food groups, the importance of hand washing, and the circulatory and digestive systems, but not whatever this film would be about. If Cecile lived with us, she wouldn't hardly tell us about food groups or hand washing. Instead she'd write poems I'd have to figure out about all those body systems, and she'd end each poem with, "P.S. Be eleven" when I had already seen my sister being born. Big Ma cooked the food in the food groups and said, "Kids are starving in Africa, India, and China, so eat every bit." She was more concerned about me washing dishes and scrubbing floors than keeping my own hands clean. Miss Marva Hendrix wasn't anything to me, so I didn't worry about what she had to tell me.

We all settled down and the reel of film rolled on.

Electric guitars picked out a lame rock-and-roll tune, and the title appeared on the screen. Our health film was about drugs. The bad kind.

First we saw teenagers at a party smoking drugs. The music was so jerky and bad, no one at the party could dance to it. Then the police came and arrested the kids, and the kids started telling the camera or us they could smoke drugs if they wanted to. Then we got the surprise of our lives. Sitting on a bed, telling us to make up our minds about the dangers of drugs, was Sonny Bono. Sonny Bono from the radio. Sonny Bono without Cher. Sonny Bono with his groovy hair and gold pajamas.

No one could have heard what he was saying because

it was Sonny Bono and we were in shock. The last place we expected to find Sonny Bono was in our sixth-grade health film talking about the dangers of drugs. He was supposed to be singing "I've Got You Babe" and "The Beat Goes On." Instead, his face looked serious, and his nose was big, even with that mustache, and he was telling us that despite what the teenagers said about drugs, he knew the real score.

We forgot about the double period of decimals and how we were upperclassmen and upperclasswomen. I forgot how much I wanted to make a better impression on Mr. Mwila. The boys were on their side of the classroom laughing, and I joined in with the girls on our side, singing "I've Got You Babe."

Mr. Mwila stopped the film and flipped on the light switch.

"You are not ready for this film," he said. And he was not angry but he was disappointed.

We took out our math notebooks before he told us to.

Chinua Achebe

When we were dismissed, I told Frieda and Lucy to go on without me. I had something to do.

I went back to our classroom. Mr. Mwila sat at his desk with a small paperback book in his hands. The book cover was mostly red and worn down, and a marker stuck out from the back of the book. When I stood nearer, I saw that the marker was the top of a photograph. Probably a snapshot of his family.

"Did you forget something, Delphine?"

I did! I forgot what I wanted to say.

"I'm sorry," I told him. "About Sonny Bono. The film." I meant to say something good and meaningful, but that was the best I could come up with on the spot.

Mr. Mwila nodded. But instead of saying how disappointed he was, he said, "Maybe a different spokesman would have made a better choice." He smiled a little.

I nodded and felt dumb and looked at his book.

There was something about the small, worn-down book that reminded me of Big Ma's Bible.

Big Ma had thrown her Bible at a white man wearing a long black coat and a tall black hat. Red Shirley Temple curls ran along the front of his ears. When I told Frieda about it, she said he was an Orthodox Jew. Well, Big Ma threw her Bible at him because he rang our doorbell the third time that week while she was studying the Old Testament. And when he said for the third time, "I'll give you all the cash I have in this satchel if you sign the deed to this property over to me," Big Ma raised her Bible like a bad boy holds up a brick at a shiny new window. "By the God of Abraham and Little David, I will smite you down!" she said. Then she threw the black brick at him and told him next time she'd have her shotgun. But I knew her shotgun was down home in Prattville, Alabama.

Mr. Mwila would never throw this small red book at anyone. But he wore it out like Big Ma reads her Bible.

He caught me craning my neck. "*Things Fall Apart*," he said, and at first I thought he had given me a warning, that everything around me would fall apart. Then I saw the book's title.

I found myself warm faced. I was failing to make a

better impression on my teacher. The last thing I wanted was to end up warm-faced or teary.

"Chinua Achebe," he said.

I touched the tip of my chin.

"Mr. Chinua Achebe," he said slower. "A fine Nigerian writer."

"Oh," I said, relieved, but now embarrassed that I had misheard him.

"Although Mr. Achebe writes about life in Nigeria, I find this book tells a Zambian story. And the longer I stay in this country, I find this book tells an American story."

"I know exactly what you mean," I said, before I actually knew what I meant.

"How so?" he asked.

He must have heard me gulp. I hoped something I had learned from Sister Mukumbu would bounce into my head and slide off my tongue. I hoped I knew what I meant. There was no straw to grasp or spin, but soon I was talking about *Island of the Blue Dolphins* and how it was about a girl alone on an island. "But you don't have to be by yourself on an island to feel alone," I said. "You can feel alone in Brooklyn or alone in Oakland." I left out that I didn't have a wolf dog, just two fighting sisters. That I didn't have a brother who was killed, just an uncle who killed the enemy.

Mr. Mwila only smiled and I hoped what I'd said wasn't too dumb.

I asked him why it took him so long for things to fall apart. He had been reading the same book since school began.

He laughed. Big. "It is my season to read this book. I know this story well. I've read it many times. But it is my season to reflect on certain passages."

I said right away with my foot planted firmly in the words I spoke, "Like reading the Bible over and over."

Then I felt a lucky spark. I must have said something right. A genuine look of surprise and agreement spread across his face.

I felt like my mind had grown to catch up with the rest of me.

It wasn't the sort of thing I'd tell Frieda or Lucy or my sisters, but I was dying to tell someone. Pa spent more time with Miss Marva Hendrix than he spent at home. And I couldn't imagine telling Big Ma her Bible and a book by a Nigerian writer had something in common. Uncle Darnell was always either out walking or lying on his bed.

That night I wrote to Cecile. If anyone understood things about books, my mother did. The night before we left Oakland she had told me how she found poetry. That the words comforted her when she didn't have a home. And it wasn't until our Bible study class recited "The Lord is My Shepherd" that I heard my mother's voice. How poetry comforted her, like the rod and staff comforts in Psalm 23.

I must have scribbled without stopping. I couldn't wait to tell her how much I'd grown that day. And that my teacher read a book by Chinwa Acheevie. That I planned to read *Things Fall Apart* as soon as I finished reading *Ginger Pye*.

My mother wrote me back.

Dear Delphine,

When you are older I want you to find Chinua Achebe. I want you to read Things Fall Apart. Don't be hardheaded and try to read this book now. Don't be hardheaded, Delphine. You are the smart one, but you are not ready. You can read all its words. Even the African words. But you will not know what Achebe is saying. It is a bad thing to bite into hard fruit with little teeth. You will say bad things about the fruit when the problem is your teeth.

I want you to read this book. I want you to know Things Fall Apart. Fourteen is a good age to find Chinua Achebe.

Nzila.
Your Mother.

P.S. For now you are eleven. Be eleven.

Sick Visit

I'd hear Pa say, "Darnell. Isn't it time you get out there and find work?"

Darnell always said, "Yeah, Lou. I'm looking."

"Look harder," Pa'd reply.

Then Uncle Darnell would go out and come back without a job.

"I don't see why you're pushing him to get a job when he's been in Vietnam fighting and saw all those terrible things," Big Ma told Pa, time and time again.

But each time Uncle came home without a job, Pa said, "You'll have better luck tomorrow. As long as you're looking." But Darnell wasn't lucky, and Pa finally said, "House is getting small, Darnell. You'll have to get a job, earn your way."

"*We*," Big Ma said, pointing to herself and Uncle Darnell, "can go *home* if this house is getting too small." She meant Alabama home.

Pa's face looked long and exhausted. "Ma."

"Don't 'Ma' me nothing," Big Ma said. "He been to war, Junior. War. Do you know what that is? Stop rushing him out the door so you can bring little Miss Cute Gal in here."

Then Pa put on his jacket and muttered about having to leave his own house. Uncle Darnell lay down on the sofa, and Big Ma threw a blanket on him and said, "You just sleep, baby."

Uncle Darnell would sleep half the day away, then walk and walk into the night. His friends from Boys' High School would come around. Friends who didn't have to go to Vietnam. Big Ma always told them he was sleeping but she'd let him know they stopped by. Two girls from his high school came by once and Big Ma told them, "Young ladies don't go calling on boys," and closed the door.

Papa hadn't left the house muttering too long ago when the doorbell rang. It was Frieda's big brother, so I yelled back to Big Ma, "It's John-Isaac," before I unlatched the chain and opened the door.

"Darnell home?"

"Yeah," I said, and let him in. I hoped Frieda had tagged

along, but it was just John-Isaac.

Vonetta had a crush on John-Isaac and came running out of the kitchen with her soapy, dish-washing hands. With dish towel in hand, Fern came running behind Vonetta. I couldn't blame them. He was looking fine in his Black Panther beret and leather jacket.

"Heard you and your sisters got some education out in Oakland."

They saluted him with power signs.

"All right, my fine young sisters."

Vonetta was giggling as if Jermaine Jackson had walked into our living room. John-Isaac had been coming over to paint model cars and airplanes since as far back as I could remember. He had even brought Frieda over when we were really little, so I could have someone besides my sisters to play with.

Big Ma came out of the bathroom to see what was going on.

"John-Isaac," she said, getting a good look at him. "Do you want to go to jail? Get shot up in the streets? Take that Black Panther mess off and act like you know better."

He put his arms around her. "Hey, Ma."

"Don't 'Ma' me nothing. Coming in here with that Black Panther stuff on. Don't spread that mess around here," Big Ma said. "We can't use it."

"We already using it," Vonetta said.

"Power to the people," Fern said.

"Slap me some skin," John-Isaac said, holding a hand out to Vonetta then to Fern. "All right, all right."

He and Frieda were so different, but probably not any more different than I was from my sisters. I figured he and Frieda were what Big Ma called "war babies." Their mother was a German Jewish lady, and their father was a black army soldier. They met when Mr. Banks was a sergeant stationed in Düsseldorf. I used to love it when Frieda told that story. Her parents' love story sounded as magical as Uncle Darnell's stories, except Düsseldorf wasn't a make-believe place, and Frieda's parents were real.

John-Isaac kissed Big Ma, who really liked it but pushed him away, just like she did with Pa and Uncle Darnell. He took off his beret and planted it on Big Ma's scarfed head and walked right by her over to Uncle Darnell, who was lying on the sofa—and Big Ma never let anyone lie on the living room sofa. Big Ma shooed us into the kitchen to finish up our after-dinner chores.

I could hear John-Isaac calling out, "Rooster! Rooster!" Then he crowed like a rooster. John-Isaac nicknamed our uncle "Rooster" because he was so "country" when he first came to Brooklyn from Alabama. And he used to do yard work before the sun came up.

"Rooster. Roo. Man. Get up."

"Let him sleep," I heard Big Ma say. "He tired."

I pushed my mop to the edge of the kitchen to see better. John-Isaac sat by Uncle Darnell like he was visiting a sick classmate in St. John's Hospital. Uncle Darnell made some "Yeah, man" sounds, but he never got up. When John-Isaac left, he hugged Big Ma for a long time. Like Uncle D was the kind of sick that didn't get better.

ThRough the GRapevine

The person who wrote "I Heard It Through the Grapevine" must have sat next to a Lucy Raleigh in school. Lucy ran over toward the girls' lunch table, her face exploding with news of some kind.

She plunked herself down between Frieda and me, and couldn't stop panting. All of that panting was meant to have us on a string. Then she'd feel extra special because she held a secret or some news. Finally she stopped panting and said, "You won't believe what I just heard."

Lucy was an office monitor. She sometimes heard what we either weren't supposed to know at all or know yet. We weren't supposed to know that Mrs. Katzman went on leave because she had a nervous condition. I guessed

Lucy's news was the other kind and she wanted to beat the office memo to our parents.

Lucy couldn't just tell us. She had to, as Pa would say, "dangle the carrot."

"You will not, will not believe it."

"Believe what?" My voice was dry and cool. I wouldn't let Lucy Raleigh get me jumping around all giddy about what she knew.

"If you must know," she said, "it's about the dance."

So much for dry and cool. My ears, along with everyone else's, must have stood as straight as a Doberman pinscher's ears. "The sixth-grade dance?" at least four of us asked at once.

She gulped and nodded. "They picked the day." The PTA hosted the sixth-grade dance. Last year the dance was held just before the spring break. Usually they waited until June.

Shouts of "When?" came from all around.

Lucy was in her carrot-dangling glory. "Guess!" she said. "It's not on St. Patrick's Day."

I cleared my throat. "Decorum. Decorum, upperclass-women," I said in Mr. Mwila's African-English accent. "And the grade-six dance shall not be on Groundhog Day."

That got a few chuckles, but none from Lucy. She hated it when I stuck a pin in her balloon. That was fine because I hated it when everything revolved around what Lucy knew and said.

"Har, har, Miss Too Cool to Care How You Dress. You won't be laughing on Valentine's Day when you're going to the dance alone."

The whole table went, "Ooh." She got me good. There was nothing I could say.

But then Frieda said really quickly, "Valentine's Day. That's less than four months away." Then everyone forgot about me and squealed as if the dance was happening tomorrow.

Just when everyone was chattering about what they'd wear, Lucy said, "Maybe your grandmama could sew you something nice to wear."

So I said, "Maybe your mama could buy you some manners at Korvettes."

"Manners. Ooh," Lucy said.

"Korvettes. Ooh, Lucy Ray." I made sure I said her name good and country like her mama would.

Sooner or later Lucy and I were bound to go from hot to cold. We always did. Then we'd be hot-and-fast friends again. Frieda was always in the middle.

Jack and the Giant

Lucy was right about my clothes. They were stupid. Even Rukia Marshall looked like a sixth grader, and she wore a cloth on her head.

Big Ma would probably sew my dress. She'd sew a dress that went way past my knees with ruffles and bows like a kindergartner's party dress.

No one would ask me to the sixth-grade dance. No one wanted to dance with a girl whose arms and legs were longer than theirs. No one wanted to dance with the tallest girl in the sixth grade. The tallest girl in the sixth grade, wearing a ruffled party dress with bows.

There was only one boy in my class who was as tall as I was. Only one.

I'd rather sit by the record player and watch everyone else dance before I danced with Ellis Carter. I'd rather stay at home and scrub the kitchen sink, the bathroom sink, the tub, and the toilet before I danced with Ellis Carter.

The way Ellis glanced at me, then turned away, I knew the feeling was mutual.

I pushed back my sweater sleeve, glad to have a ticking second hand I could rely on. Good old Timex. Eight seconds . . . the warning bell! Just another five minutes until dismissal.

The only boy who would ask me to dance was on the other side of the Golden Gate Bridge, riding down a hill on his go-kart.

I wasn't like Vonetta and Fern. I couldn't go dreaming about Hirohito Woods getting on a plane in his Sunday pants, knocking on my door in time for the sixth-grade dance. I couldn't go dreaming about a big white flower he'd put on my wrist, and him telling my father he'd bring me home by nine o'clock. I couldn't go imagining that he was a really smooth dancer and we'd look good together and he'd get me punch and sit on the sidelines with me when Principal Myers played lame songs on the record player. I wouldn't go imagining how my friends would all want to dance with him, starting with Lucy Raleigh, but he'd say he'd only dance with me.

***

Hirohito Woods was like a make-believe boy, and not a real boy I knew. He wasn't even my pen pal. You couldn't be a pen pal if you didn't write letters to each other. And you couldn't write letters if you didn't know where to send them.

I closed my eyes and remembered that he and his mother lived on Magnolia Street near Mean Lady Ming's Chinese takeout. The fourth house on the block. I sat on the steps in his yard reading my book. He chased Vonetta and Fern around his yard. There were plants like green rubber roses in clay pots, but they weren't rubber. They were real and filled with water if you pinched their petals.

I saw everything about Hirohito Woods's house in my mind except the house number.

But I knew his name. That he lived in Oakland on Magnolia Street. Maybe that was enough for the telephone operator to help me call him person-to-person from a phone booth. I didn't dare call the operator on our telephone in the kitchen. If Big Ma wouldn't let girls from Uncle Darnell's high school come calling, she wouldn't hardly let me use the telephone to call a boy long-distance.

All I needed was about a dollar and a half in change to talk to Hirohito.

I found thirty cents. I needed to borrow one dollar and twenty cents in nickels, dimes, and quarters. No pennies. Most of the money in the Jackson Five Madison Square

Garden concert jar was mine and now I needed to shake some of it out.

I went inside Vonetta and Fern's room while they did homework. The mummy jar was right on Vonetta's desk.

"I need to borrow money," I told her. "One dollar and twenty cents."

Vonetta lifted her head. "We can't spend that money," she said. "Not a penny."

"Not a nickel," Fern said.

"That money is for—" and before I knew it, they were singing the Jackson Five's "The Love You Save" but they changed the words so it was all about saving money for Madison Square Garden.

I wasn't happy my sisters had made up songs I knew nothing of, but I wasn't about to poke out my bottom lip and pout.

"I need that money for stamps to write to Cecile."

"And to write to Hirohito," Vonetta said. "Your lover man."

"Your dreamboat," Fern said.

"Dear Hirohito, I miss you more than . . ."

"I miss mosquitoes."

They congratulated each other on their rhyming.

At first I meant to stretch the truth, but then I out-and-out lied to my sisters.

"I'm writing to Cecile. I need airmail stamps."

"To send love letters to your kissy, dreamy lover man?"

I hated that they were right. That I wanted the money for Hirohito. I hated that they were making kissing noises that smacked the insides of my ears.

"I put more money in that jar than the two of you. If you want me to put my birthday money in there, you better shake out some of that money right now." I called on Cecile for some of her meanness. And grown. I needed to sound good and grown.

Vonetta took the jar and hugged it to her chest. Fern ran over and hugged herself around Vonetta and the jar.

"That money is for Jermaine and Marlon."

"And Michael."

Then they started singing their own money-saving song, and Fern made up a part about how they had to save the money from me.

I could have wrestled that jar from them in nothing flat. I felt my face burning and my throat choking. I wanted to cry but I didn't want them to see me cry. Or know that they could make me cry. Maybe I didn't have what Cecile had. I turned to go to my room and heard Vonetta say, "We killed the giant. Like in 'Jack and the Beanstalk.'" Then Fern said, "And we have the golden goose." And they shook the mummy jar with all of my money in it and sang, "The giant is dead, the giant is dead, the giant is dead."

Twelve

Most kids couldn't wait for the end of October and filled their dreams with Halloween candy. I couldn't wait for the last week of October because of my birthday. I tried to reach midnight with my eyes wide open so I would know when I turned twelve. Twelve was worth staying up for. Six different numbers went into twelve. There were twelve days of Christmas, although we only celebrated Christmas Eve and Christmas Day. Twelve was equal to one dozen, and a dozen was a good amount for Oreos but not so good if you were on the losing side of throwing down the Dozens on the playground. I'd lost a round of Dozens to Danny the K last year when I'd said, "Yo' mama," and he said, "You don't have a mama." I tried to stand up to him as best as I could but he got me and all I could say was, "So?" Some things were good to add on when you turned twelve and some things were good to leave behind. Like playing the Dozens in the school yard.

I tried hard to stay up but Papa knew I'd turned twelve before I did. Either late Friday night or early Saturday morning, he placed my birthday money and my allowance on my dresser next to my talcum powder and my Timex. Six dollars and fifty cents.

I hoped a card from Cecile would arrive on my birthday. A made-up card with a "Turning Twelve" by Nzila poem printed on it that Big Ma would roll her eyes at. I wouldn't have minded if it came without birthday money. I just wanted it to come. I wanted to know what she thought about me turning twelve.

I just didn't want to be propped in the window, watching for the mailman the way Big Ma used to wait on letters from Uncle Darnell. My sisters and I walked down to the candy store on Fulton without Uncle Darnell. I promised to spend some birthday money on them and to contribute to our Jackson Five concert savings. That was enough to keep them happy.

Vonetta surprised me by saying, "Not too much money, Delphine. We don't need candy. We need thirteen more dollars for the concert at Madison Square Garden."

Fern was quietly confused. She didn't dot Vonetta's words with agreement like always. A bag filled with wax lips, Jolly Ranchers, and Pixy Stix was the very thing that made Fern skip to the candy store. She loved her little Michael Jackson, but she hadn't figured on giving up so much to see him.

I hated to admit it, but I was looking at a whole new Vonetta. She was determined to be the best saver imaginable, determined to see her precious Jermaine and Marlon in person, and determined to prove me wrong about her being irresponsible. Normally I'd poke fun at her but she was doing so well, and I didn't want to be the mean giant that she wished was dead.

Fern yanked my jacket and said, "You'll get us some candy, right, Delphine?"

"Yeah," I said.

Across the street I saw Ellis Carter and Danny the K kicking a soda can. They wore their baseball shirts and were on their way to the stadium at St. Andrews Playground. Danny the K poked Ellis, but Ellis pretended not to feel it. They must have seen me across the street with my sisters. I turned into the candy store as if I hadn't seen them. While Vonetta and Fern charged to the counter lined with fishbowls of penny candy, I stood at the door and watched Danny the K push Ellis into the street and almost into a car. Tall and dopey Ellis flapped his arms like a bird and hopped back onto the sidewalk. He slugged the K, and the K laughed and danced around him. Before they could catch me watching them clowning around, I found the magazine rack.

I refused to look at *Highlights for Children* because I was now twelve. Instead, I planted myself before the four teen magazines that Mr. Mack's Candy Store carried. *Seventeen*, *'Teen, Young Miss*, and *Tiger Beat*. Magazines that talked about first dates, the right clothes, teenage TV stars, singing groups, and acne cream, although I didn't have a need for acne cream.

In the lower right-hand corner of the *Tiger Beat* cover was a small photograph of Michael Jackson's face. I grabbed the magazine and thumbed through the pages, searching for the Jackson Five. Something we'd all enjoy. Vonetta would change her tune about spending money if there was a big enough picture of Jermaine and Marlon.

I leafed past pages of TV stars, rock-and-roll groups, and pop idols. At last, at the back of the magazine, I found a single black-and-white snapshot of Michael, but no Jackie or Tito. Not even Jermaine and Marlon. Michael was fine for my sisters, but I was twelve. And tall. I wanted a picture of Jackie, or one of Tito playing his guitar.

Vonetta was right. If we wanted to see Jackie, Tito, Jermaine, Marlon, and Michael, we'd have to save our money for tickets to Madison Square Garden. I shoved *Tiger Beat* back in its spot and picked up *Seventeen* and fanned through it. Not one article about how to hot-comb without wearing that smoky hot-comb smell to school.

When I paid for Vonetta and Fern's candy, the store

owner—the same one who'd been selling me pencils, pens, writing pads, envelopes, and erasers since I don't know when—said, "I ought to charge you for reading my magazines."

"You can't charge her for reading your magazines," Vonetta said. "It's her birthday."

I wasn't about to let Vonetta come to my rescue. "Twelve" said, "I didn't read. I looked." Then "Oakland" added, "When there's Afros and black faces on the cover, I'll buy one."

"Power to the people," my sisters said.

"Free candy," Fern added, instead of "Free Huey."

When we came home, there wasn't any mail at all from Oakland. Wishing for a card from Hirohito would have been like wishing for make-believe. How would he have known it was my birthday? How would he have known where to send a birthday card? But I expected a card from Cecile. Even though I'd lost a round of Dozens to Danny the K, my mother wasn't make-believe. She was real. And she knew where to send my birthday card.

At least Big Ma had the house smelling like barbecued chicken and lemon cake. Enough to drown out the good-for-us stink of mustard greens. I threw my arms around Big Ma, happy that we'd be eating barbecue in late October when Big Ma only smoked and barbecued meat in the summer.

Big Ma pushed me off of her and said, "Go on and wash up so you can help me with this mixing bowl."

I had to race my sisters to the bathroom but Fern managed to squeeze past Vonetta and me.

"It's my cake batter," I said. "I get the first lick."

"Not if I beat you," Fern said.

"Surely won't," I said, pushing her away from the sink.

"I'll beat you both," Vonetta said, and just dashed her hands on top of ours in the sink, wiped them on the towel, and ran.

"Stop that clonking!" Big Ma hollered. And when all three of us stood before her, grinning and ready to lick the bowl, she declared us "a bunch of wild hyenas running loose in the jungle."

I took the wooden spoon. Vonetta and Fern used their fingers.

Every now and again, I checked the window to see if the special delivery mail truck had rolled up to our house. Then I stopped checking.

That night we had more of a birthday celebration than I was used to. Uncle Darnell seemed like his dimpled, jokey self. Like he wasn't war tired and like he hadn't had a fitful night. He put Fern on his feet and danced around with her, although she had grown since he'd last whirled her around while Nat King Cole sang. He said he might have a job at the post office. Just waiting on a call. That made Pa happy, but honestly, Pa was happy to have his Miss Marva Hendrix sitting next to him, flashing her perfect teeth. Everyone sang the regular birthday song to me and then my sisters and I sang our version just before the wishing and cake cutting began.

Happy birthday,
Eat cake
Leave room for ice cream, too!

Happy birthday,
Eat cake
Leave room for ice cream, too!

Happy birthday, Delphine,
Happy birthday to you.

Happy birthday,
Eat cake
Leave room for ice cream, too!

Our song was easier and snappier to sing than the "Happy Birthday" song we sang at parties and in school. And you could do the cool jerk while singing it. Then all of us were dancing except for Big Ma, who yelled, "Cut this cake before the candles melt all over it!"

Uncle Darnell said, "Make a wish."

There was a world of wishes but I knew the one I wanted. And I knew it couldn't be. Not even if it was my birthday. I knew my mother would never be here. That my mother and father would never make our house happy together. Knowing these things came with having twelve candles to blow out, plus the extra candle to grow on.

"I want to see the Jackson Five at Madison Square Garden," I said. Then I gave Vonetta my five-dollar bill. I didn't pass it under the table, but gave it to her so Miss Marva Hendrix could see.

Vonetta ran to her room, got the mummy jar, and pushed the five-dollar bill down the slot. "You just want to see Jackie Jackson at Madison Square Garden."

"And Tito," Fern said.

Uncle Darnell leaned over and said, "Is that who you're digging on? Jackie Jackson and Tito?"

I knew my uncle was back to being himself. Dimples and jokey. I felt warm but I refused to sink my face down, embarrassed like I would have been back when I was eleven.

I said, "Yeah. I like Jackie and Tito."

"Only one you should like is your pa," Big Ma said. "And your uncle."

"Band of singing hoodlum boys," Papa joked. I knew my father. He'd only half joked about the Jackson Five. I'm sure he didn't appreciate Vonetta, Fern, and me screaming over a group of boys, no matter who they were. Miss

Marva Hendrix must have known Pa almost as well as I did. She felt sorry for him and took his hand.

That night Fern got out of her bed after she'd been tucked in. She came into my room while I was in the middle of reading *Johnny Tremaine.* "You weren't supposed to tell your wish, Delphine." She stood there with her tiny fists balled and banging at her sides. To her, I had broken the rules on wishing. To her it was serious. Fern still believed in all those things.

I told her to go to bed. I sounded grown.

Hee Haw Square Dance

Ellis Carter slid into his chair. He turned toward me, about to speak, but then his face went dopey and reddish. Then he turned away, hunched himself over, and dropped his head on his desk. That didn't last very long.

"Head up, Mr. Carter."

He reluctantly rolled his chest and head to sit up straight, face forward.

"Much better," Mr. Mwila said as if Ellis had done something stupendous. "Now you look alert and ready."

Danny the K said, "He's ready, Mr. Mwila. Right, Elly May?"

Ellis turned even redder and I felt a little bad for him.

Even though the K was Ellis's best friend, the K was

the first one from the boys' side of the room to call him Elly May Clampett after the big blond girl on *The Beverly Hillbillies*.

"Mr. McClaren, would you like to return to your corner?"

Since September, the K had made a few visits to the corner next to Mr. Mwila's desk. "No, sir," he answered. The K spoke politely, like he had a Big Ma of his own who had taught him to say "yes, sir" and "no, ma'am." And I'll bet she and Danny's mama were tired of Mr. Mwila calling their house to report on his fooling around. Mr. Mwila believed in dialing up parents. He called that an "opportunity to involve the home community with the school community."

Mr. Mwila announced, "Today we shall continue our studies on the upcoming presidential election by forming discussion groups."

Rukia raised her hand but spoke before she was recognized. "We're going to be talking for the entire period?"

"Organized discussion," Mr. Mwila said.

"So that means—"

He stopped her this time. "We're in grade six and not in kindergarten, Rukia. We raise our hands and wait to be recognized."

The boys loved seeing a girl get reprimanded and couldn't hold it in. "Oh, snaps," came flying from their side of the room. Mr. Mwila seemed eager to get on with our new project. He let the boys' outcries pass.

"We shall break into groups of four," he said. "Since we're equally matched, we'll have two boys and two girls in each group. You'll have one minute—sixty seconds—to find your group members or I'll pick your group." He pushed back his jacket sleeve to see his watch. Starting—"

Lucy Raleigh grabbed Frieda—who I wanted as my second girl—and headed straight to Michael Sandler. Frieda gave me a "sorry" glance from across the room. Michael S. had James T., and their group was set. Evelyn, who was Michael S.'s sort-of girlfriend, made a rhinoceros sound and took Theresa over to Anthony and Ant's group. Evelyn made Anthony get rid of Antnee and take Upton instead. It was like square-dancing on *Hee Haw*, except with mostly girls running around from group to group calling out the allemande lefts and dos-si-dos. The girls had the right idea. Pick the boy who caused the least amount of trouble. Who did all his schoolwork and didn't spend the period with his nose in the corner.

I sat at my desk watching the class move and swirl. I finally lifted myself up to see where I would go and decided on Enrique and James W.'s group. Carmen and Monique were already on their way over to their desks.

Mr. Mwila clapped his hands together once and said, "Time." Without skipping a beat he pointed to Rukia, then Danny the K, and said, "You're in this group," meaning with Ellis and me, although we weren't together.

"Quickly. Quickly," he said.

I raised my hand but Mr. Mwila wagged his finger and shook his head to stop me. "The election is next week and we have much to accomplish." Then he wrote subjects on the board and began to talk about the "objectives for our group discussions and presentations."

I was stuck. No surprise fire drill alarm would sound in time to rescue me from having to look at, let alone talk to, Ellis and the K. Rukia wasn't so bad, just annoying. I glanced at Lucy and Frieda smiling on the other side of the room. It wasn't fair. I was supposed to be with Frieda.

Once Mr. Mwila outlined our aim for this period, he sat at his desk and opened his little red book. *Things Fall Apart.*

I glanced at my Timex. Thirty-two more minutes until our group broke up and Rukia and the K moved back to their own desks. Thirty-two more minutes until Ellis and I could look away from each other.

I felt myself all wound up inside like the innards of a clock. Instead of teaching us about the election, Mr. Mwila expected us to teach ourselves. Occasionally he cleared his throat and said "Decorum" to a group that was getting out of hand. At least they were excited about their discussion and had chosen their subjects. What I wouldn't have given to be anywhere but with my group. All around the room, groups were talking about voters' rights, the electoral college, the two-party system, and Richard Nixon versus

Hubert Humphrey. We weren't talking about anything.

Danny the K snapped a rubber band at Ellis. Ellis, whose head went back down on his desk, said, "Quit it," and closed his eyes. Rukia said for the sixth time, "Can I switch groups?" Danny answered, "Can you?" Or he'd say to her because she was a Muslim, *"Asalamu alaykum.* Pass the pigs' feet and the bacon." Then she'd raise her hand and ask again, "Can I switch groups?"

"We need a subject," I said.

Ellis shrugged. Danny the K aimed another rubber band, but Mr. Mwila cleared his throat again and the rubber band disappeared.

If I were at home with my sisters, I would pick our subject and tell Vonetta and Fern which subtopics they would discuss, case closed. But I wasn't at home.

Danny the K finally said, "We already have a subject. The presidential election. Let's talk about that."

"That's the overall subject," I said. "We need a specific subject and then subtopics." I pointed to the list of subjects on the blackboard.

"Ooh. Specific," the K said.

Rukia said, "We should open the textbook and look up what's on the board. Then we'll pick something."

I whirled my hand around helicopter style at all the groups talking and said, "They didn't look up anything. They're having discussions."

But as usual, we had nothing to say to one another.

Then Rukia said, "I know what our specific subject can be. We can talk about what would happen if a woman ran for president of the United States."

"What?" That was all I could say. I had never heard of anything so far-out. And nowhere on the board did it say *"women running for president."*

Danny the K laughed. Ellis sat up. Sort of.

"Yeah. That would be funny," Danny the K began. "We could say, 'Mrs. President. How will you win the war in Vietnam?'" With his eyelashes fluttering, the K said in a high-pitched warble, "'I'll bake the Vietcong a nice apple pie.'" He and Ellis laughed it up.

I said, "The subject is 'What if a woman ran for president?' Not 'What if your pie-baking mama ran for president.'" And before I knew it I had thrown down the glove like they did in *The Three Musketeers*. Instead of fencing, there was a war of the Dozens between Danny the K and me.

So he said, "At least my mama can shake and bake. Your mama can't bake a pie because your mama don't exist. Your mama's the invisible mom."

He couldn't shut me up like he did last year. I said, "My mother don't bake no pies. My mother writes poems about the revolution. My mama exists. Your mama's invisible."

And while all of that was going on and the room was getting quiet, Mr. Mwila appeared at our group, looking down mostly at me.

Rukia saved the day by saying, "We have our subject, Mr. Mwila. Women running for president."

But it was Ellis who shocked me. Shocked us all. He pointed to the blackboard and said, "Under eligibility."

Instead of saying that was good, Danny the K said, "Yeah, Elly May. Under eligibility."

Mr. Mwila congratulated us on our topic. He said we had a lot of catching up to do because the other groups were already writing out presentation drafts. Then he wrote a slip for Danny the K and me to spend the rest of the period in detention.

Suited to Be President

I was onto Mr. Mwila. He thought because Danny the K and I sat in detention, that we'd talk to each other like the grade-six upperclassmen he told us we were.

Danny's "you make me sick" faces met my "too cool to care" blank stares. The only thing I cared about at the moment was if Mr. Mwila saw this as an "opportunity" to call my house. The more I thought about Big Ma getting that phone call, the more I regretted being in detention with Danny the K. I missed being in class where everything was happening. Plus I had to save our group from Rukia Marshall and women running for president. If New York City had never had a woman as our mayor, how would the country elect a woman to be president?

The detention aide got up from her desk and sternly warned us, "Mr. McClaren and Miss Gaither," to be on our best behavior while she left the room for a few minutes.

I glanced up at the big clock, whose minute hand never seemed to move in spite of the second hand winding around and around. I looked down at my Timex. Four more minutes before I could join my class. And what if Pa decided I couldn't go to the Jackson Five concert because I was shouting "Your pie-baking mama!" in social studies, like a dice-throwing hoodlum?

I thought of how I wanted the one thing that seemed hardest to get. I wanted Mr. Mwila to think better of me.

Danny the K pursed his lips. I thought to make kissy smacks, but he would be the last person on this earth to blow kisses at me. At first I only heard pitchy whispers stabbing the air around me. Then I saw Danny's spit shooting through his puckered lips. The whispers grew louder. Clearer. Until there was a tune. A tune I knew.

With his eyes sparkling like beady marble shooters, Danny the K whistled that stupid TV dolphin song, and he dared me to do something about it.

I crossed my arms and looked away.

Danny whistled louder.

I stared up at the big clock. My "too cool to care" face wasn't holding up. I pinched a chunk of my arm and gritted my teeth. My ears were getting hot as he leaned forward.

The detention aide had not yet returned. Danny the K got up from the bench and danced to the tune of the *Flipper* song. Danced and whistled. He came closer, probably hoping I'd push him away so he could push back. He wanted me to start it.

I kept looking up at the clock, praying the minute hand would strike 1:40 and the bell would ring. I let out a sigh to pretend I didn't care, but he whistled even louder. Until he got me with his stupid spit, right below my eye.

I wiped my face and turned away. Turned away when my fists were ready. So ready.

Danny knew it. His whistling got louder and he leapt like a ballerina.

Then Principal Myers walked in.

Mr. Mwila had not called our house yet. Big Ma would have given me an earful the second I came into the living room, where she sat in her chair, resewing Pa's shirt buttons. I didn't want to stew over the detention note that she or Pa had to sign. I got it over with and took the mimeographed letter out of my book bag. The smell of purple ink swirled up my nose when I unfolded the bright white paper. The writing on the paper was blurry after too much recopying but Big Ma would be able to read it. This was the second detention letter I had brought home. The first was from punching Ellis in the jaw last year.

I braced myself for either the scolding or the sting of Big Ma's right hand. I expected to get one thing or the other. Or both.

"What did you do now, Delphine?" At least this time she asked what it was all about first. My sisters and I weren't supposed to bring trouble in the front door. Especially not from school.

I spoke plain and clear. "I got into an argument in class with Danny McClaren."

"You're in class to learn from the teacher," Big Ma said. "Not to be arguing with some know-nothing boy."

I heard myself while I retold the whole thing. It sounded silly.

Big Ma never looked up once from her sewing. When I finished telling, she said, "Women are too busy to be running for president of the United States. What are they teaching at that school? Woman president. Hmp."

"My teacher might call." Might as well let the other shoe drop.

"Let him call. I'll straighten him out."

Big Ma was funny, as in hard to figure out. She had loved President John F. Kennedy but hadn't wanted a Catholic president. She loved keeping up with the Kennedys in the supermarket gossip papers but also loved wagging her finger at them.

I remember the president's brother, Robert F. Kennedy, came to Bed-Stuy a lot—before the riots and after. His visits were always in the newspapers. Back in spring, when I was in the fifth grade, just months before he, like his brother, was assassinated, Big Ma put on a church outfit to hear the senator speak. Vonetta, Fern, and I asked if we could go with her but she said it wasn't a meeting for kids. I learned later that plenty of kids had gone, and Rukia Marshall had posed for a picture with Senator Kennedy. That color photograph became her show-and-tell.

Well, Big Ma had gone down to Friendship Baptist Church to hear Senator Kennedy tell the black people they were American citizens who deserved decent homes, decent education for their children, safe neighborhoods, and opportunities. But Big Ma talked more about taking off her glove to shake a Kennedy's hand than she talked about his speech. You'd have thought Big Ma would've been baking cookies for the "Vote for Bobby" office on Fulton Street, the way she talked and talked about Senator Kennedy. But she said she wouldn't vote for him because his hair was too long and he let people call him Bobby and not Robert. He was too young, talking about changing things in Bedford-Stuyvesant and in every other ghetto. She said that while that sounded good, and the people hollered and clapped for him, he was still a rich, young Catholic boy whose daddy made millions selling liquor.

Instead, she planned to vote Republican for Richard M.

Nixon who, to Big Ma, was more suited to be president of the United States than a Catholic boy with hippie hair—or any Democrat, for that matter. She and Pa talked back and forth about that. After the assassination, Big Ma told Pa not to waste his vote on the Democrats. Instead of fixing things for the Negro race, Richard Nixon would win the war in Vietnam, clean up the country of its long-haired, drug-smoking hippies, and get those black militants and bean-pie-selling "Mooslims" in line. He would make America great.

Pa would say that Richard M. Nixon wasn't good for black America, but Big Ma would say, "Life for colored folks is how it's been. If Reverend King couldn't fix it, it can't be fixed. Only Jesus can give colored folks their rightful place, although Reverend King came close."

That's what made Big Ma both funny and hard to figure. When she looked at Richard M. Nixon, she saw what a president should look like. But I bet you wouldn't have caught Richard M. Nixon at Friendship Baptist Church on Herkimer Street.

Big Ma put down her sewing needle and signed the note.

"Don't get caught up in foolishness, Delphine. You just study your lesson. Gradurate"—she said it with an *r*—"and maybe you can go to college. Be a schoolteacher. Something nice like that."

Then I said the thing I'd never have said to my revolutionary poet mother. Still, I knew it was the right thing to say to Big Ma. I took the signed detention slip and said, "Yes, ma'am."

Sweetie and Honey

Pa came home early enough that night to have dinner with us, but he didn't come alone. While we sat at the table and Vonetta filled in Miss Marva Hendrix on how good of a saver she was, I heard Pa in the kitchen, taking a tone with Big Ma I had never heard him use. "Get used to it, Ma," I heard him say.

I pretended not to hear and so did Miss Marva Hendrix, but we both knew what was simmering in the kitchen besides gravy. Big Ma didn't care for Miss Marva Hendrix too much, but Pa refused to yes her like he did when they'd had words about Cecile.

My stomach knotted and rumbled from hunger and funny feelings. I wanted Pa to win the fuss going on in the kitchen because he was my pa. I wanted Big Ma to win because she didn't punish me for getting myself in detention. And I guess I was a little mad at Pa because he never fought for Cecile to stay.

Vonetta went on and on about all the money we were saving and how she made sure Fern and I didn't waste our money buying candy, airmail stamps, and mooning over boys in Oakland. Then she ran to her room, brought out the jar all taped up, and shook it for all of us to hear. Even Uncle Darnell perked up when he heard the coins shaking. Then she put her mummy jar back in the room. Miss Marva Hendrix couldn't say enough nice things about Vonetta and how she was doing a good job.

I put up with Vonetta because we were almost halfway to Madison Square Garden. In less than six weeks we'd see Jackie, Tito, and the rest of their brothers live onstage. That was worth Vonetta crowing over her job as our saver, and boy, did she crow.

Big Ma brought out the pork shoulder and burnt gravy.

Pa shooed Vonetta out of the seat next to his fiancée. He pecked Miss Marva Hendrix on the forehead, and Fern said, "Ew. Mushy and gushy."

Big Ma said, "Let's not have any of that mushy and gushy at the table."

Then Pa gave Miss Marva Hendrix a real smack on the lips, and instead of being mad or sickened, I surprised myself and laughed out loud.

"A mercy, a mercy. Bless the table."

When Miss Marva Hendrix added, "And all of us gathered here," she didn't know that wasn't the blessing. Just Big Ma telling Pa to say grace. Pa said, "Amen. Let's eat," and that was that. Then Big Ma gave a look to Pa. The same "mark my words" look that she gave when he spared me from the whipping rod. Pa acted like he didn't catch Big Ma's look.

If Uncle Darnell was being his jokester self, he would have gone over to one of us and planted a big smack on our lips. But Darnell sat curled over, sniffling back snot, his lids droopy. No matter how much rest they gave him at that hospital in Honolulu, he stayed sick and sleepy.

And he wasn't lucky. The post office hadn't called about the job.

Miss Hendrix looked at Pa like she knew something. Pa looked at her. I could tell by their eyes that they were having a full conversation grown-ups have without saying words. I figured it was grown stuff, which made me want to know what they were keeping from us. Neither Pa nor Miss Marva Hendrix gave me much to work with, but sooner or later, I'd come upon a clue and piece things together.

The not-knowing made me dislike secrets, and then I remembered I had one of my own. I hated keeping things from Pa, and since I was surrounded by my family—minus Cecile; minus Miss Hendrix, who wasn't family yet; and minus Uncle Darnell, who was there but wasn't his old self—I decided I might as well tell Pa about the day.

"Pa," I said.

My father had shoveled in a mouthful of rice and gravy. He looked at me, his eyebrows arched, urging me to go on.

"I got into trouble at school today."

Vonetta and Fern "oohed." This would be the place where Uncle D was supposed to say something funny to keep Pa from getting mad, but Uncle D just sniffled. And Pa didn't seem too mad.

"Delphine, what did I tell you about fighting with boys? You're too old for that." He turned to Miss Hendrix and said, "Boys at school always teasing her."

"Th'ain't the problem," Big Ma said. "Problem's what they're teaching at that school."

Vonetta and Fern sang another chorus of "ooh."

I spoke up. "I was arguing with Danny the—Danny McClaren."

"About what?" Pa asked.

I couldn't say the Dozens part. Not at the table. I said, "Our social studies group needed a subject, and Rukia said women running for president of the United States and Danny said—"

"Something dumb," Vonetta chirped.

While I was busy glaring at Vonetta for interrupting me, Miss Marva Hendrix clapped her hands together and said, "That's a marvelous subject for social studies. Right on!"

Vonetta and Fern had to say it too. "Right on!" And Big Ma scolded them for talking ghetto at the dinner table, half blessed as it was.

"Now, now, sweetie," Pa said to Miss Hendrix, the same way he told Fern, "Now, now baby girl. Ain't no bogeyman in the radiator pipe."

Miss Marva Hendrix didn't hear him "now-nowing" her. She said, "Stick to your guns, Delphine. Women belong in politics just like men."

Big Ma said, "Women belong in their homes taking care of their families, and schools shouldn't be teaching them any different. Who'll take care of everything if young women are running around trying to be dog catcher and councilman?"

"You, Big Ma!" Fern said.

Everyone laughed. Uncle Darnell smiled a little.

But Miss Marva Hendrix thought she was having a discussion. She said, "There's no better way to look out for families than to make sure the government remembers the needs of children, women, and poor people. Who better to speak for children than women?"

"The men who take care of them," Pa said without hesitation. "The men who put a roof over their heads. Food in their mouths." He stuck his fork in his potatoes.

"I know, I know, honey," she said.

Sweetie. Honey.

"But sometimes men forget these things," she said. "They think about getting more, making their empires bigger, war."

"Tell it," Uncle Darnell said.

But Pa said, "Some things gotta be."

"Some things gotta change," she said back.

They were talking to one another and not us.

"If you ask me," Big Ma said, "they ought to stick to teaching arithmetic in schools. Arithmetic. Home economics. Reading and history. Not all this jaw-jerking about women running for president. A woman running for president. When pigs fly over Alabama."

"Pigs in the air!" Fern said as if she could see them.

Uncle Darnell smiled. His eyes were closed.

"There are a lot of women making noise in politics," Miss Hendrix said.

"Noise, for sure," Pa said. But Miss Hendrix ignored him.

"There's a lawyer named Bella Abzug. She has a good head on her shoulders and a loud mouth—and I mean that in a good way." Her eyes twinkled at Pa.

I'd never seen a lady lawyer, but I knew what she meant about having a loud mouth. Like Angela Davis had a loud mouth. And Kathleen Cleaver had a loud mouth. She was talking about people who weren't afraid to say things.

"Only thing Bella Abzug's good for," Big Ma said, "are

her big old hats. Hmph. Quiet as it's kept, she's only wearing those hats to catch the eye of a husband."

Miss Marva Hendrix laughed politely. She could have let Big Ma have her say or changed the subject. Instead, she said, "I'm working on the campaign to elect Shirley Chisholm to be the first black congresswoman."

I thought, Congresswoman? Was that a real word? But I didn't want to accuse Pa's fiancée of making up words. Instead, I said, "You work for Shirley Chisholm?" I knew her name and saw her on the local news. But I didn't think her campaign was for real. I didn't think any men would vote for her. I knew my Pa wouldn't.

"I volunteer," she said.

Big Ma said to Pa, "Do you hear that, son? Are your ears and eyes open? Teaching foolishness in school, and bringing it home to this half-blessed table."

It was funny. I felt one way when I sat down at the table and a different way before we had dessert. I couldn't make up my mind about women with big mouths running for president or about Miss Marva Hendrix. I certainly didn't know what to think about my father.

True-Blue

I shouldn't have been surprised by the angry words that came from our kitchen. Pa and Big Ma argued a lot lately. This time, Pa's voice was firmer. Although I couldn't hear all of the words, I could hear what Sister Mukumbu called an "ultimatum." Once you give an ultimatum, you have to mean it. You can't pull back. Sometimes your "or else" is all the power you have and you can't be afraid to do what you threaten to do.

Pa said, "He better find work," and Big Ma said, "He's sick." Pa said something like, "The house is too tight," then Big Ma said, "You can't" and "He's your brother." Then I heard Pa say that having Darnell around the girls—us—wasn't good. That was when he gave Big Ma his ultimatum:

"If Darnell don't get cleaned up, he's got to go."

Then Pa walked out into the dining room in time to catch me. "Delphine, that wasn't for your ears. Go on and do your homework."

"I did my homework, Pa," I said, careful how I spoke up. "Big Ma told me to come peel potatoes."

"Go on and do what your grandma asked."

I "yessed" him and went into the kitchen. Big Ma was wiping her face with her apron.

"What you want?" she asked.

"Peel potatoes," I said.

She'd forgotten. She had Uncle Darnell on her mind. And Pa.

"Wash your hands," she said like she was still arguing with Pa. I didn't tell her I had already washed them in the bathroom. I squeezed some Ivory dishwashing liquid on my palms and turned on the kitchen sink.

Having Uncle Darnell home was supposed to make us all happy. My sisters and I prayed to keep him safe when he was in Vietnam. Big Ma got on her knees every morning and prayed for an hour. Most of her praying was for Uncle Darnell.

The only thing I knew for sure was that Pa didn't want his own brother in the house.

I knew that Uncle Darnell wasn't himself, but was that a reason to stop loving him? Was it all right to stop loving someone you're supposed to always love?

I didn't know if Cecile loved us when we were born. She let Vonetta cry and cry in her crib. She left Fern before she could know Fern. She still left me even when she let me be with her while she wrote poems. And Pa. She left Pa.

All I knew about my parents was that Pa took Cecile in when she was sleeping on a park bench. They had us, and Pa painted the walls every time Cecile wrote on them. Then she left us after Fern was born. Pa wore his long face every day after that for seven years.

I think love wears out, and Papa's love for his brother had worn out now that Uncle Darnell rattled and hollered in the night like a ghost. His bones stayed cold and his nose stayed runny. He didn't wolf down his food or dance lame old dances like he used to. Maybe because Uncle Darnell wasn't his whole self but was like a ghost. Maybe that's why Pa couldn't love him like he used to.

Vonetta didn't notice, or she pretended she didn't notice, but Fern had stopped clinging to Uncle D. Fern heard him hollering at night like the boogeyman howling and rattling in the radiator pipes. She was afraid of him.

One day Uncle D was sort of fine and the next day he wasn't, even though he said, "Everything is everything." But he didn't sing "everything is everything" like it was a Stevie Wonder tune. I think Pa knew his brother was being changed by the war when I showed him that letter back then. I think Pa didn't want me to be afraid of my uncle or his letters. I think Papa loved him then, when he was in Vietnam, but he didn't seem to love him anymore.

Big Ma was different. Her love was like her hate. It was true-blue. Big Ma would never love my mother. Even though my sisters and I came from Cecile and looked like her in different ways. Big Ma would not love Cecile, but she would love us, even when she was whipping us. Even when she was calling us a bunch of untrained chimps.

Big Ma would love Uncle Darnell even when he was rattling around like a ghost on her couch. Even when Papa couldn't love him, Big Ma would. Big Ma's love would stay true.

Change of Seasons

I felt it in my fingertips while we walked to school that morning. This November promised to be chillier than past Novembers. Leaves had already turned yellow and had fallen everywhere. Soon our classes would all file into the auditorium while we waited for our teachers to come and collect us. For now, we ran around on the playground until the lineup bell rang and our teachers stood at the head of our lines.

I couldn't help but notice a change in more than the seasons. The clusters of girlfriend groups where I would have fallen in with Frieda, Lucy, and whoever they stood with were dotted with the Jameses. Two Michaels. Enrique. Upton. Anthony, but not Ant. I couldn't believe it. The boys weren't tagging girls on the back and running off, but talking with them. It felt like it was happening behind my back. Suddenly the boys were acting human and were able to be around girls without clowning or starting trouble. Not with me. Or Rukia. But they were all talking to each other. Or maybe because I noticed two or three boys talking to two or three girls, it seemed like the whole world had changed in an instant and I was on the outside watching it change. Not that I had anything to say to the boys in my class. And I had no intention of standing near Danny the K or Ellis. They kept their distance from me, which was fine by me. The way Danny the K glared at me, I could only guess his mama had given him the whipping of his lifetime the other day.

Lucy turned and saw me. She grabbed Frieda's hand, came running over, and did a less goosey version of her Lucy-goosey dance. Frieda rolled her eyes. Then Lucy waved a card in her hand to the beat of her dance and shoved it in my face. She sang, "I got it, I got it, I got it, OW!" She was a female James Brown screaming and sliding back and forth.

There, before my eyes, was a real Madison Square Garden ticket with THE JACKSON FIVE IN CONCERT printed on it. I was both excited and turning green inside and out. All I could do was look.

"Mine is on my dresser," Frieda said. "At home where

the wind can't blow it away."

Lucy kept dancing and showing off her ticket. "You've got yours, right, Delphine?"

"Not yet," I said, "but almost."

"Almost? Almost?" Lucy went on as if I had said I almost had polio. "There's no such thing as almost. Not with the Jackson Five! Girl, are you crazy?"

I didn't see what the problem was. December was still a few weeks away. "We have half the money," I told them.

"You better get a whole ticket," Lucy said.

"Yeah, Delphine. They're going to be sold out." Frieda was almost as dramatic as Lucy, except she really cared and wasn't showing off. "Mom made John-Isaac get my ticket. And he's taking me."

"And we're sitting together," Lucy said. But Frieda shot her a look, like she didn't want me to know that. Lucy didn't care.

"I have mine," Evelyn said.

"Me too," Monique said. Theresa and Carmen also chimed in.

Rukia said she wasn't going. Then Lucy said no one had asked her, so I said, "It's a free country. She can say what she wants to say." Frieda said nothing.

I was glad we didn't have group discussion, but instead worked silently on writing our presentations. The boys

stayed on their side of the classroom—except for Ellis—
and we stayed on our side. The next day we continued our
work on the presidential election project. Thanks to Miss
Marva Hendrix, I brought in a Shirley Chisholm button
along with her leaflet. Even though Miss Shirley Chisholm
wasn't running for president, she was running for a seat in
Congress. That was enough to show that a woman could
hold a high office in politics. If enough men and women
voted for her to be elected as our congressman, then who
knew? Pigs might be flying over Alabama.

When I practiced my points and conclusion for Big Ma
and Pa that night, Big Ma said she couldn't believe they
handed out grades for that. Pa said I spoke well. But neither of them said my points made sense. For the first time
in a while, Big Ma and Pa seemed to be on the same side.

I showed my materials to my group. I was glad I at least
had something to contribute. Rukia had so much information on the first woman governor and senators from
the encyclopedia, she couldn't stop talking. She said her
mother had helped her. Mrs. Marshall was a principal at a
different school. No wonder Rukia believed women could
be president. Her mother ran an entire school.

Ellis had a piece of paper that he'd written his points
on, but he kept it crumpled.

Danny the K had his big mouth open. "It will never
happen," he said.

The more he spoke, the more I thought, Yes it will. I wasn't sure if I believed a woman could be president, but if Danny the K said it would never happen, I had to believe the opposite.

Danny the K didn't dampen Rukia Marshall's far-out thinking one iota. Rukia said, "Since you guys don't believe a woman can run and we do, why don't we do our presentation like a debate?"

"That's dumb," the K said.

Ellis shrugged.

I said, "That's a smart idea."

"Shut up, Stretch," the K said.

"You shut up," Rukia said.

Then Ellis said, "Debate. You mean us two against you two?"

It wasn't that I didn't think a woman could run the country. I didn't think enough people would vote for her. There were more people out there like Big Ma, Pa, and Danny the K than there were people like Rukia and Miss Marva Hendrix.

I knew what would happen with Miss Shirley Chisholm on election night. She would run. Some people would vote for her and then she'd lose. Folks would say, "Nice try for a woman," and "Nice try for a black woman." Then we'd get a man for our congressman. A white man.

"We'll slaughter them," the K said.

"We're prepared," I said. "We'll debate you under the table."

Ellis Carter uncrumpled his loose-leaf sheet. To my surprise, he had a lot written on it.

Another Drumroll

We all gathered in Vonetta and Fern's room as we had been doing since Pa insisted we save our money to earn our way to the concert.

"Drumroll, please," Vonetta said.

Instead of a drumroll, Vonetta handed Fern the Jackson Five concert jar, and Fern shook it round and round so the quarters, dimes, nickels, and pennies made a metal whirling against the glass, softened by a few bills. We probably wouldn't have the best seats in the Garden, since we'd have to buy our tickets late, but at least we'd be there. So what if Lucy, Frieda, and John-Isaac bought their tickets early and had seats closer to the stage? Close enough that Jackie Jackson could spin around, stop, pose, and then point dead at them and be looking in their eyes while I'd be just another girl screaming from way, way back. Way, way high. I could still say I saw the Jackson Five live, at Madison Square Garden.

Vonetta added up our deposits on her savings chart and signaled for Fern to stop shaking the jar. "According to my tally, we've saved a grand total of . . ."

That was Fern's cue to give the mummy jar another drumroll.

"Ten dollars and seventy-three cents," Vonetta said. "That means we only need—"

"One dollar—"

"No, Delphine! I got it. I got it," Vonetta said. She closed her eyes to do the subtraction. "The zero becomes a ten . . . minus three, equals seven . . . and the other zero becomes a nine, minus seven . . . so it's one dollar and twenty-seven cents!"

We cheered and jumped and sang "I'm Going Back to Indiana," messing up the song lyrics to announce that we were going to New York City to see the Jackson Five at Madison Square Garden. We couldn't make those words fit no matter how hard we tried, but that didn't stop us from squeezing, dropping, and rhyming the words.

We danced until Big Ma told us to stop that noise-making "like a herd of stampeding hippos." That we should use that energy for praising the Lord. And that was enough to start the other two praising Jesus for

198

helping us to save and I fell in with them, praising and stomping. Then Big Ma said, "That's not the meaning of 'Jesus saves.'" But it was too late. "Jesus saves for the Jackson Five" was the only praising going on in our room. Even Big Ma had to laugh.

We had soon worn ourselves out and I heard the rumble of the Wildcat. It needed a new muffler that Pa said he didn't have money to fix. I think Pa just liked the way the Wildcat growled and rumbled like a crouching animal about to strike. I think Pa liked his Wildcat just fine.

I looked out the window. Pa and Miss Marva Hendrix were coming up the steps. He carried a large suitcase and she carried a smaller one. Their hands were joined.

When I opened the door, they stood there smooching on the porch. I was flustered and went to close the door, but they broke apart and Pa said, "No need for that." He was smiling and I felt stupid. "Go on to the car and grab a box from the backseat."

I didn't run to the car like he told me. I just stood there. Miss Marva Hendrix kissed me on the cheek, then followed Pa.

Pa called out, "Darnell! Darnell!" but Uncle D wasn't home.

I went out to the car to get a box from the backseat. There were a few boxes on the seat, and smaller ones on the floor. Boxes marked *MH BOOKS. MH RECORDS. MH SHOES. MH CUPS.* I grabbed one marked *MH BOOKS.*

She had a few of those.

Pa was still asking where Darnell was. He needed help to bring in the rest of Marva's things, he said.

Big Ma said, "He's out like you told him. Looking for work." She put her hands on her hips and hooked her head toward the kitchen, their arguing place. "Now, son, we need to talk."

But Pa held up his left hand. His left hand with a gold band around his ring finger. Miss Marva Hendrix leaned into him.

"Ma. Darling daughters," he said. "I'd like you to welcome my wife into our house."

I was both shocked and not surprised. Shocked because we were hearing about it just like that. Not surprised because Pa wanted to be with Miss Marva Hendrix forever.

I was all right. Sort of. But Big Ma's hat feather could have knocked her flat on her back.

Miss Marva Hendrix was beaming, showing us her gold band.

Big Ma needed a moment. The hands that had been planted on her hips were now fanning her face.

I looked over at Vonetta and Fern. They wrapped their arms around each other. Finally Vonetta spoke. "You had the wedding, Pa?"

"Without us?"

I hadn't seen anything more pitiful than my sisters' 'bout-to-cry faces.

Pa couldn't see how hurt they were. We were. He was happy to bring Miss Marva Hendrix into our house for good.

"We didn't need a wedding," Pa said. "We went to the courthouse."

Miss Hendrix poked him in the ribs. It was meant to be playful, but there was too much shock and hurt and silence in the room and she wasn't blindly happy like Pa. "You see," she scolded him.

"You're married?" Big Ma asked. "Without family?"

Miss Hendrix felt bad. "Mrs. Gaither," Pa's wife said. She had sense enough to not call Big Ma "Ma" or whatever she called her own mother. And it hit me: I knew nothing about her. Other than how she dressed, that she believed in Vonetta before I did, and that she thought women could run things.

"My lease is coming up on my apartment and—"

Big Ma put a smile over her real face and said, "Welcome to our home. Your home." She turned to Pa and said, "Congratulations, son."

I had never heard Big Ma's voice sound like that. Like someone who was sick but had to pull herself up out of bed anyway.

I followed my grandmother in saying the right thing. "Congratulations, Pa." I turned to my father's wife. "Congratulations, Miss, Miss . . ."

"Missus," she said, smiling, and she kissed me again.

Vonetta and Fern came outside with me to finish bringing Mrs. Marva Gaither's things inside the house.

Mrs. Marva Gaither. It didn't sound right.

"I told you they weren't having a wedding," I said.

"Shut up, Delphine," Vonetta said.

"Yeah. Shut up."

They were hurt and mad, but we moved quickly bringing Pa's wife's boxes inside. The night air was chilly.

Dear Cecile,

    I thought I should tell you that Pa has married Miss Marva Hendrix. I don't know if you care, but I thought you should know. They didn't have a wedding and Big Ma didn't bother to make them a fancy wedding dinner. Vonetta and Fern are getting over not being flower girls.

    Pa's wife is nice, smart, and she believes women can run for president. She's all right. But Pa would have asked you to come back to Brooklyn if you said you loved him and us.

Your daughter,

Delphine

P.S. I am twelve.

Dear Delphine,

I know how old you are. I was the first to know you were with me. In me. Growing. I counted the weeks and months as you grew. I waited for you to come. A birthday is more than cake and presents. It is the day you come into the world. The day you come into being. I know your birth day.
I know your father is married. I know he is happy.
All you need to know is the world is big and you are in it. Study your lessons. One day you'll see the world.

Your Mother.

P.S. Still, be eleven.

Taste of PoweR

Rukia asked Mr. Mwila if our group could have more time. She had five written pages of information and she wanted to use them all. He commended her on her thoroughness, but said the idea of presenting a subject is the ability to focus. "Pick out your strongest points and use your allotted time to present them. Two minutes for each speaker, and no more."

Danny the K said they were ready to blow us to smithereens.

Ellis asked if we wanted to go first, but I did one of his numbers. I shrugged.

"You're pro woman president," he said.

"So," I said.

"So . . . you know." He could barely look me in the face. "It's *pro* and con. So you should go first."

I shrugged again.

"Yeah," Rukia said. "You do the first argument. Then Danny goes next. Then me and then Ellis." Her eyes lit up and she said, "Then we ask the class to vote by show of hands. Should a woman run for president or not?"

"Hey, that's good," I said, thoroughly surprised.

Ellis nodded and said, "Okay."

"We already know who's going to win," Danny bragged. "It's in the bag."

I went first. Two minutes seemed to go on forever, but I had my points ready. I had practiced. I knew each point by heart, although I kept my paper in front of me. And before I knew it, I was saying my conclusion, and Danny had begun his argument on why women could not make important decisions about war or about the prices of oil and gas. Then he said in his conclusion that women were better cooking with oil and passing gas. Mr. Mwila had to give one hard hand clap and shout, "Decorum, class three," to settle things down. Rukia spoke jackrabbit fast to jam in as many women leaders in her two minutes as she could. She ended by saying that we'd already had a woman president during World War II. That Eleanor Roosevelt ran the country when her husband, the president, was sick. Then Ellis gave his reasons why men were made to be leaders and women were not. He almost sounded like Pa.

Mr. Mwila congratulated us on our presentations. He said we all did a fine job presenting our subject and making our arguments. Then we voted.

All the girls said women should run for president if they wanted to. But all the boys raised their hands to vote "No." Then Michael S. gave Lucy one of those Michael S. looks, and Lucy changed her vote. The boys won.

Before Danny the K could say something clowny, Mr. Mwila wagged his finger and said, "Upperclassmen, be gracious." Then he turned to me. "An excellent presentation, Miss Gaither." He smiled warmly and added, "Well done, Miss Marshall."

When we returned to our seats, Ellis smiled a little and said, "Sorry, you . . . sorry."

On Tuesday night, Big Ma finally had something to cheer about. She got the president that she prayed for. Pa wasn't too pleased that his candidate, Hubert Humphrey, had lost the election. He said no black person in the US should have voted for "Tricky Dick Nixon." Big Ma said she wasn't black. She was colored. Then Vonetta said, "And Negro on Sunday." And Fern said, "A Sunday Negro. Surely is." Uncle Darnell said he hoped someone good would run in the next election when he was old enough to vote.

Mrs. was down at the Shirley Chisholm campaign

headquarters celebrating her candidate's win. Big Ma couldn't believe the people in New York voted Shirley Chisholm in as their congressman. She said, "Where's your wife, son? Out there politicking and not taking care of her husband. That Shirley Chisholm already breaking up homes."

Pa paid Big Ma no mind. He and I stayed glued to the local news, hoping to spot Mrs. at the campaign headquarters reveling in the victory. Much to my surprise there were hundreds of people cheering on our new congressman, when I thought it would be just a handful of people.

Or was that *congresswoman* like *upperclasswoman*?

Pa tried to be nice about it. He said, "It's good to have a black person representing the people."

Big Ma said, "She black, all right." And I knew how Big Ma meant what she said, and that it wasn't nice or Christian-like. My sisters and I were about the same color as our new congressman. Woman.

I knew it was a good thing. An incredible thing. But I wasn't sure if her victory made a dent. Was it real power, like the Black Panthers mean power, or was it just a taste of power? Like Vonetta being the saver. Vonetta was doing a good job, but it didn't mean everything had changed. She washed dishes and tried to scrub the bathtub, but I still had to get after her to hang up her school clothes instead of throwing them on the floor.

Never on a Sunday

Saturday night, just before Vonetta and Fern jumped into a tub full of Mr. Bubble, Big Ma hollered, "Get your clothes ready for church. I don't want to hear no chicken feet scrambling in the morning."

She meant that she didn't want to hear Vonetta and Fern tearing up order to find slips, socks, barrettes, and gloves. I used to put everything on hangers for them to make my life easier on Sunday mornings, but not anymore. If Vonetta and Fern could do chores, they could put their clothes together for Sunday. I still ironed their cotton slips and their dresses but they had to hang their clothes and polish their own shoes, and that was always a mess.

Pa and Mrs. watched Wilt Chamberlain and Bill Russell try to stop each other from scoring baskets. Mrs. seemed to like basketball and knew what a foul was. Wilt the Stilt had put one over on old Bill Russell when she turned to Pa and said, "Sweetie, we're going to church too, aren't we?"

Pa never talked during a basketball game. He just watched. He stared straight ahead and said, "Hmhm."

"Good!" she said, giving him a smack on the cheek. He paid her no mind, but she kept on talking. "It's been a while since I've gone to church, so why not?"

On that one, Big Ma, not at all surprised, went, "Umhmm."

Mrs. didn't care that Pa was glued to the Lakers and the Celtics game or that Big Ma was just a step from calling her a backslider and a heathen. She got up and went charging into her and Pa's bedroom the way Vonetta and Fern ran through the house, and came back to the living room flag-waving a green suit with a wide collar before Big Ma. "What do you think?"

I always thought she and Pa were around the same age but now she looked younger than my father. Much younger.

Big Ma said, "That's a smart number, all right. I'm sure you'll look nice in it, small as you are."

Mrs. was not one to shrink from a compliment. "You got that right!" she hollered.

Big Ma said, "All you need is a hat."

Mrs. said, "A hat doesn't go with this hair." She shaped her hands like a globe around her Afro. She was right. No hat would fit over that big, curly Afro.

"You're a married woman, Marva," Big Ma said. "A married woman wouldn't step foot in church on a Sunday without a hat."

"This one will," Mrs. said. She wasn't being mean. Just stating a fact.

Then Pa unstuck himself from Wilt Chamberlain and Bill Russell to say, "Marva. You'll put a hat on your head. Ma, get her one of yours." He said it minus the "honey." Then Mrs. started to say something, but Pa cut her to the quick and added, "Or we're not going." And that was that.

Big Ma was happy that night.

Come Sunday morning, Mrs. was dressed and ready for church, with a pinned-on hat, a shiny black purse, and black gloves that crawled past her wrists. Pa didn't want to go.

"A man works," Pa said, fixing his tie. "He need to rest."

Mrs. fixed her mouth to say some "sweetie" thing but Big Ma was louder, and this time, faster.

"God worked and rested," Big Ma told Pa. "The least you could do is praise Him on His day."

That was all Vonetta and Fern needed to get the morning praise going.

Pa was already in his suit. He just wanted to voice himself.

It seemed funny how things had gotten turned around. Before, Pa stayed home and Uncle Darnell went to church with us in his black suit and kept a pair of white gloves folded in his pocket. He ushered along with John-Isaac, the only Banks member of Friendship Baptist. Frieda and Mrs. Banks went to temple on Saturday, and Mr. Banks didn't attend a service of any kind.

Uncle Darnell was asleep in his bed with a cold. He had only gone to church the first Sunday that he was home from Vietnam.

When we got to church, I saw John-Isaac right away, looking all revolutionary in his black suit and beret. Even though Uncle D was back in the US, I knew John-Isaac missed him the same way we did. John-Isaac probably hoped Uncle was back to being his old self, wearing his white gloves and ushering and flirting with girls. When our eyes caught, John-Isaac flashed me a power sign and I returned it quickly before Big Ma could see. The head usher said something to John-Isaac and the beret came off and was tucked inside his jacket.

Big Ma knew what she was talking about, as far as hat-wearing was concerned. Plenty of eyes were on Pa's new wife, and I was sure that Mrs. appreciated Big Ma telling her how to dress. Our church was filled with unmarried women who had placed home-baked casseroles, bread puddings, and cakes in Big Ma's arms so Pa would know they were good cooks and available for marriage.

After the service, Pa went up to the pastor to introduce his wife, and Big Ma was all smiles. Big Ma's smile soon flattened when the pastor said—his face still glazed in a smile—"You know you're not really married unless you're married in the house of the Lord." He said that with enough church ladies within earshot. Big Ma was fit to be tied, but she held it in.

Pa spoke up in his warm, smooth way. "Reverend," he said, "State of New York said she's Mrs. Louis Gaither. I'm sure the Lord will come around."

The pastor smiled and patted my father on the back and said, "Good man. Good man."

Usually after service we went down to the basement and had cake, fried or baked chicken, and string beans. Then we went to the noon service. This Sunday, Pa said, "We'll see you back at the house, Ma," and he told us to get a move on, and we were walking down Herkimer Street headed back to our house. Us three girls, Mrs., and Pa.

One service wasn't enough for Big Ma. She would be at Friendship Baptist until six.

I hoped Pa would treat us all to a late breakfast at the diner, but we went straight home. Pa swatted Mrs. on the backside and said, "Get in that kitchen and show us what you can do."

Mrs., who was what Big Ma called a "now generation" woman, didn't put up a protest. She even laughed and took Big Ma's little black hat off her smushed Afro. She'd used a lot of hairpins to make the hat stay on.

"Scrambled eggs and bacon coming up!" she said.

We couldn't wait to get out of our Sunday clothes. "Hang 'em up!" I called to my sisters.

I doubted Mrs. could cook like Big Ma, but I knew she could scramble some eggs and fry bacon without burning them. Even if her cooking wasn't any good, I was hungry and would eat every scrap.

Then I heard screaming coming from Vonetta and Fern's bedroom. I ran. Pa and Mrs. followed.

Vonetta was on the bed hollering, "It's all gone! It's all gone!" at the top of her lungs like she hollered in her crib when she was a baby. The mummy jar had been unscrewed, the tape stripped off, the crayoned picture of the Jackson Five torn. A few pennies and dimes were on the floor, but the quarters, the nickels, the five-dollar bill, and all of the single dollars were gone.

Vonetta and Fern were joined in a crying, sobbing heap.

"The money. The concert money," Vonetta choked it out. "It's gone."

Their room seemed small and tight around us. Pa looked at Mrs. and said, "Darnell."

I said, "Uncle Darnell wouldn't take it. He wouldn't."

Pa said, "Hush, Delphine. You don't know nothing about this."

Mrs. went to Vonetta and wrapped her arms around her. Fern ran into me and threw her arms around me tightly. I could feel her rib cage heaving in and out.

"You don't know how sick your uncle is," Pa said. "You don't know nothing about this kind of sick. It's not for children to know."

That was when I knew. I knew what Pa was saying. I'd never seen it before to know for sure, but it slowly formed a picture in my mind. My uncle wasn't a ghost rattling around the house. My uncle was on drugs.

My Girls

"Don't worry, girls," Mrs. said. "I'll replace the money you raised."

Upon hearing that, Vonetta began to dry her eyes with her shirtsleeve and Fern shouted, "Yay!" Then Pa said, "No, Marva honey. You can't do that," and my sisters wailed, "Papa! Papa!" and "Yes, she can," and "Surely can, Papa. Surely can." I would have wailed along with them, but I knew Pa's mind was set. Once set, Pa didn't bend.

"Hush." He spoke firmly. My sisters and I heard the promise of a whipping behind that kind of hush. Vonetta's and Fern's wailing simmered to whimpering.

"But, sweetie," Mrs. said, "they worked so hard. They held up their end."

Pa told her, "I don't expect you to understand, but these are my girls and I'm raising them right."

Except for the whimpering, there was a silence you not only heard, but one you could see on Mrs.'s face. The way it changed.

"*Your* girls? *Your* girls?" The silence stood between them. When Pa made no move to correct himself, Mrs. turned on her heel and was gone. First their bedroom door slammed. Dresser drawers opened and slammed. Not long after that, the front door slammed.

Pa didn't go chasing after her like they do in movies. He stayed cool. "She'll see right." Which meant he was right and she'd come back after she cooled off.

Cecile didn't come back.

The girls whimpered on. I whimpered with them but mine was stuck in my throat and only showed in my raised eyebrows.

"Not everything can be fixed," Pa said.

Between sobs, Vonetta said, "But she was gonna fix it."

"She was, Papa," Fern said.

"Listen here," Pa said. "I need you to hear what I'm saying even if you're too young to understand. You can't have everything in life that you want. Some things are meant for you. Some things just aren't."

What did being young have to do with—

"But what about working hard, Pa?" I said. I'm no back-talker but my mouth opened. With my sisters crying, I became one of those loudmouths that Mrs. talked about. I couldn't stop. "Vonetta and Fern did chores. Vonetta put the savings jar and the chart together. She kept count over the money. She made sure we saved our money and didn't spend it on everything we wanted, and we wanted things."

Come what may, I had to speak up for my sisters.

"All of that's good, Delphine," my father said calmly. "But that's what you're supposed to do. Help out at home. Save your money. Work toward goals. Here's the part you're too young to understand," he said to me especially. "You don't get paid for that. The reward is in the doing."

He was right about being too young to understand. How can you work hard and get nothing? I just couldn't "yes" him because I didn't understand and I didn't agree. But I knew I had another point and I had to make it.

I said, "Papa, you said if we did those things you'd give us half of the money to buy the tickets. That was your word, Papa. What about keeping your word?"

My point was good. I knew I'd won. He should have "seen right" in everything I said.

He nodded and said, "I know, Delphine. I know." Then he said nothing for a while and I knew, I just knew, he'd seen right and I had saved the day for my sisters and me.

But then he said, "If you girls get over this disappointment, you'll get over the rest of those to come."

And then Vonetta yelled, "I'm never doing any chores or saving, EVER!"

The silence around that was brief.

"Vonetta." Papa was cool. So cool I stepped in front of her. "You won't get none today but never raise your voice to me in my house. You got that?"

She sniffled and nodded, but Papa wasn't taking no sniffling and nodding.

"What was that?"

"Yes, Papa."

He got up. "Y'all girls cry about it tonight, but come tomorrow I don't want to hear none of this sniffling and moaning over those finger-popping hoodlums."

Then Fern jumped forward. "Michael is not a hood-lum!" Her fists balled at her sides.

Papa, who was at the door, turned around, and Fern jumped behind me.

We just sat on Vonetta's bed. The three of us. We sat and cried all night.

I'm Not Muhammad

I woke up feeling worse than when my head had hit the pillow the night before. I had gone to bed knowing my uncle was a thief who would steal from his nieces. That my uncle wasn't sick from war, but sick from drugs. I tried to sleep, but all through the night I heard moaning. It wasn't my uncle rattling around, but Big Ma saying, "My son, my son. Give me back my son, Lord. Bring him home."

Except for the evergreens, there wasn't a leaf on a tree that morning. Vonetta, Fern, and I walked to school, none of us saying a word. I didn't feel like talking to anyone when I got to the playground.

My classmates were all gathered in one oblong mob

with Frieda in the center. She seemed to be doing all the talking, and it seemed odd because that wasn't how Frieda was. Talk, talk, talking so everyone would be fixed on her. Frieda was cool and never needed a crowd around her.

Then Michael S. looked up and did a head jerk my way. Frieda and Lucy moved toward me and brought the crowd of six-three with them.

Frieda stepped closer to me and said, "Hey. Is everything all right?"

My hard night's sleep must have shown on my face. I tried to make my expression bright but I'm no actress. I just said, "Sure." Had it just been Frieda and me alone, I would have told her about yesterday and Uncle Darnell, but they were all there, hovering. Waiting. I said, "Everything's okay."

Frieda Banks, with everyone there, practically sang, "Your grandmama came by last night looking for Darnell and she was crying, Delphine. I felt so bad."

I looked dead in Frieda's face.

I thought, Did I hear right? Did I hear what I thought I heard? Did I hear Frieda, my friend, my friend since we were little, trying to make me feel bad in front of the class? Did Frieda just snap the Dozens at me, talking about "your grandmama"?

I was mad enough to push Frieda into Lucy and send half my class falling like bowling pins. I was mad enough, but I didn't push her. I didn't want to be walking the paddle mile or bringing home a third detention slip from the office. I said with the right amount of neck-rolling, "Frieda Banks, if you care so much about why my grandmother was crying, then you can go to Herkimer Street and you can ask her."

It wasn't snappy, but I tossed my head and walked away.

How do you ignore a person who sits directly to your right? Someone you always shared a smile or an eyeball roll with? By the end of the first period, I became an expert at ignoring my used-to-be friend, Frieda Banks. If I accidentally caught her eye, I stared past her like I was using X-ray vision to see through the wall to her right.

Frieda tried to apologize all day and sent Monique over in chorus with notes I wouldn't read. At least she knew better than to send notes through Lucy. I only rolled my eyes while Monique sputtered Frieda's apology. Then Frieda told Rukia to tell me she was sorry and wanted to talk but Rukia said, "You might be the mountain but I'm not Muhammad." Only Rukia and I knew what that meant. If Muhammad won't come to the mountain, then the mountain will have to come to Muhammad.

I could carry a chip on my shoulder for a year and a day, but by dismissal I began to feel bad. Bad on top of the bad I was already feeling over everything else going on at home. Mrs., gone. Uncle Darnell, a thief. Drug sick. Gone. My sisters crying. Big Ma moaning. And no Jackson Five concert at Madison Square Garden.

I figured I'd let Frieda off the hook when I saw her alone. But when I was walking toward her, Danny the K called out to me from down the hall, "Delphine! Delphine!" When I turned, I saw them—Danny the K and Ellis Carter, but Ellis was walking away from him, like he didn't want to be anywhere near his friend. The K called out to me again, but now I heard him clearly. He wasn't saying my name. He was shouting, "Dope fiend! Dope fiend!"

Quick-Fast-in-a-Hurry

Our house didn't smell like cooked meat or vegetables when I opened the front door. Big Ma hadn't started cooking, and she didn't show any signs of getting started. She sat in the living room with her big Bible in her lap. She didn't yell at Vonetta, Fern, and me to wash up, hang up our clothes, or get our lessons started like she'd been doing every day after school. We did those things anyway.

Big Ma never made quick-fast-in-a-hurry food. She made food that needed washing before it touched a knife, pot, or pan. Or she made beans that soaked overnight and simmered with neck bones for a good part of the next day. And stewed meat in heavy enamel pots, with bay leaves and carrots and potatoes that soaked up gravy. Big Ma cooked food meant to stick to your insides and keep your belly full. She cooked food that took time.

If cooking hadn't started by two or three o'clock, we'd have to eat quick-fast-in-a-hurry, which were the meals I cooked. Franks and canned pork and beans. Fried chicken, boiled potatoes, and frozen green peas. Sometimes I made spaghetti with catsup and any kind of cut-up, leftover meat from the night before. The few times when Big Ma was sick, Uncle Darnell brought in a pizza pie. Big Ma never liked that and always got well the next day so we wouldn't get used to take-out food.

I said, "Big Ma, you want me to get something washed or cooking?" I spoke gently. She acted like she didn't hear us when we came in.

She shook her head and said, "I'll get to it in a minute."

So I went to my room and brought my books into my sisters' room, where we did homework. I'd rather look up and help Vonetta and Fern than have them run in and out of my room with every problem. Vonetta hadn't been doing that lately. Once she got the hang of figuring out money she saw numbers as money to be saved for the concert. Except now there was no concert.

Fern had only two sheets of homework and both sheets looked easy. Still, she sat for a long time and wrote and erased, then wrote and erased again.

I tried to not think about losing Frieda and why she

went telling everyone about Big Ma knocking on her door crying and Uncle Darnell being sick from drugs. I tried to not think about Danny the K yelling out "dope fiend." I did my homework, but I spent more time watching my sisters do theirs. I wished I had their homework.

Keys jangled. The front door opened, then closed. We put our pens and pencils down but only Fern ran to the window.

"Too early for Papa," I said.

"No Wildcat," she said.

It was Darnell, I thought.

Vonetta must have thought the same thing. She jumped up and ran out of the room. She had it in her mind to shake or punch Uncle Darnell like he was Fern or me. She was going to shake him until all of the money he had taken fell out of his pockets. I didn't tell her or Fern what was wrong with him. That he used the money up and couldn't be giving it back.

It didn't matter if "old" Uncle Darnell had come back to us and was holding tickets to the concert. From what I knew, drugs didn't let go of you just like that. Not those kinds of drugs. Being sick from drugs wasn't like being sick from a cold, although Uncle D could never seem to be rid of the cold he always had. I didn't know much, but I knew you didn't smoke drugs one day and leave them alone the next.

Vonetta needed to let go of seeing the Jackson Five. Pa didn't mean for us to go to Madison Square Garden in the first place. If he did, he would have let Mrs. replace the money Uncle Darnell stole from the savings jar. I didn't really understand the lesson Pa was trying to teach us about disappointment, but I knew he wanted us to forget all about the concert and the Jackson Five.

When we ran into the living room, we didn't see Uncle Darnell looking sick and full of "sorrys." It was Mrs. walking into the living room. She had come back.

Vonetta and Fern ran and jumped on her. Just like they had done with Cecile at the airport when it was time to leave Oakland. They squeezed her and begged her not to leave.

I was glad to see her too, but not as glad as they were. I had Uncle Darnell on my mind. I said, "Hey."

She said, "Hey, Delphine."

Big Ma sort of looked up. "You're back, Marva?"

Mrs. said, "I'm back, Mrs. Gaither."

We let Big Ma sit in her chair with her big Bible while we cooked. Mrs. could cook, but she was no Big Ma in the kitchen. She cooked like me. Quick-fast-in-a-hurry. I hoped my father knew that.

A week passed and Uncle Darnell hadn't come home.

Big Ma asked Pa at Thanksgiving dinner, "Did you go looking, son?"

He said what he said yesterday: "I drove around. Went by his friends. No one seen him."

I knew she'd ask again. She always did.

"Good riddance," Vonetta said into her napkin. I kicked her under the table. She had it coming but said, "Cut it out, Delphine," anyway.

"You both cut it out," Pa said.

"Son, you'll go and look again tomorrow?"

From across the table, Mrs. shook her head in tiny yesses, urging Pa to say he would.

Pa said, "Ma . . . he'll come home when he's ready."

"What if he won't?" Big Ma said.

I glared at Vonetta: *Don't you dare.*

She glared back.

Fern said, "I saw that!"

No one paid Fern any mind.

"He's a man," Pa said. "He's not a little boy. He's got to find his own way back."

Big Ma slammed her hand down hard on the table. "But he can't, son. He can't. He's sick."

Then Mrs. pulled Fern's chair back and told her to get down and said, "Delphine, take them back to their room."

We went.

"Some Thanksgiving," Vonetta griped. "I didn't finish eating my turkey."

"Or the yams."

"We'll eat later," I said, and made the sign for "shh." We

could hear Pa and Big Ma arguing. Then feet stomped and a door slammed.

That Thanksgiving, I was thankful that only the bedroom door slammed. And not the front door.

Every Good-bye

When I was four, my grandmother seemed like a giant.

The flowers on Big Ma's muumuu now seemed bigger, just like the comfy chair she had been sitting in for the past seven years now seemed bigger. The nurses and doctors whispered their secrets on *General Hospital* while the soap opera organ played a tune full of worry. Big Ma seemed to shrink before my eyes.

The box of Oreos on the table meant she had left the house and gone to the store while we were at school. I called Vonetta and Fern to get their after-school snack. Two Oreos and a glass of milk each. They came running with their school shoes still on, said, "Hi, Big Ma," and went straight to the Oreos and milk in the kitchen. Big

Ma didn't yell about "a pair of unbroken broncos kicking and neighing to get at a plate of cookies." When she didn't say a word, I went out to the living room to check on her.

Big Ma looked up at me and said, "Your uncle." Her eyes were big and sad.

"You've seen Uncle Darnell?" I asked. "He's been here?"

Vonetta must have heard Uncle's name and came out into the living room, her hands and lips all cookied up. "He's here?" She patted her foot. "Wait till I get my hands on him."

"Yeah," Fern said. "Just wait."

"Darnell's gone." Big Ma spoke plain. Soft. Like nothing mattered any longer. Not the cookies. Not Vonetta's foot-patting. "Darnell's gone."

I asked, "Gone? Gone where?"

Big Ma's tears welled up. "I must have been at the store. . . ." She looked down at a piece of paper on top of her Bible. It was a sheet from my letter-writing pad, which meant Uncle Darnell had been in my room. I took the paper.

"What did he say, Delphine?" Vonetta asked. Now her hands were placed where her hips would grow in. She hadn't stopped patting her foot.

"Yeah. Read it."

So I read it aloud:

"'I have to go, Ma. I'll be all right. Kiss the girls. Everything is everything. Darnell.'"

Then Vonetta said, "I don't want your stupid kiss, you sicko, runaway thief. Keep running for all I care."

Color returned to Big Ma's face. And then some. Before Fern could tag on a "surely anything," Big Ma said, "Bring me my belt," and Fern jumped away from Vonetta and next to me.

I said, "Big—"

"Bring me my belt."

I looked at Vonetta. Stupid, fast-mouthed Vonetta, and there was nothing I could do to save her. I sped to Big Ma's room. There wouldn't be any group discussion and debate on this subject. If I'd opened my mouth or questioned Big Ma, she would have gotten up out of her chair. And if she got up, it wouldn't be to whip Vonetta but to get me.

I opened the closet and took down the hanger that four of Big Ma's belts swung from. The best I could do for Vonetta was to choose "Wanda, the Good Switch" over "Lightning." We had all gotten a taste of Lightning. Me, Vonetta, and Fern. One lash was all it took before you saw lightning on a clear day. Lightning was a maroon color gone brown. Its thin leather strap stretched from being fastened around the waist to the last hole, and was now a hardened leather with a blinding, mean snap.

Wanda, the Good Switch was newer and had a little padding to it, if you were lucky to get its softer side. I brought Wanda out to Big Ma.

A whipping didn't come without what Big Ma calls "a wisdom." According to Big Ma, a whipping and a wisdom went together. The wisdom is what you're supposed to remember long after the sting of the whipping became a memory.

"Don't—you—ever—open your mouth about your uncle, or call him out of his name!"

Don't you ever. Three. Three lashes across the legs. Fern jumped to dodge each one, although she was far away from Wanda. But Vonetta. Poor Vonetta. Even Wanda's goodness couldn't save her.

When it was over, I hugged my sister, who smelled like Oreos, the saltiness of tears, and hot, crying breath.

She tried to push away from me. "Leave me alone. Leave me alone." But I wouldn't. I didn't leave her alone to cry and sulk and hope for darkness to come and think bad thoughts about Big Ma and Uncle Darnell. I hugged her until she hugged me back and got all her crying out.

Dinner was quiet. Pa didn't say anything about Darnell leaving. Big Ma didn't say anything about Vonetta needing the whipping she got. Mrs. didn't fill the air with talk.

Saturday morning, Big Ma had on her Second Sunday outfit. She wore no gloves. Her cheery feather slunk to half-mast and lay flat against her hat. Pa had walked her suitcases down to the Wildcat and was putting them in the trunk.

"Come on, Vonetta," I said. "Let's say good-bye to Big Ma."

Vonetta crossed her arms.

"Stop acting like a baby," I told her.

"Yeah, baby," Fern said. "Quit it."

Vonetta uncrossed her arms. "Don't call me a baby, baby."

"You're the baby."

"You are."

And they kept at it but Pa was ready to go. I looked out the window. He was pumping the foot pedal, and the Wildcat was growling.

I knew the best way to get my sisters moving. I said, "Beat you down to the car!" Then I took off.

Behind me was the scuffle and clomping of shoes. We came bounding toward Big Ma on the porch. She yelled, "Stop that running like a band of gypsies!" We didn't care. We circled her, and hugged her, and said our good-byes.

Vonetta didn't say she was sorry but she did hug and kiss Big Ma good-bye.

Mrs. was still in her housecoat. It was eight a.m. If Big Ma had a word or two to say about how late Mrs. slept on Saturday mornings, she kept it to herself. Instead, Big Ma said, "Keep an eye on my girls."

Mrs. said she would.

And then more hugging and kissing went on until Big Ma said, "Let's stop all this carrying-on, making a grand Negro spectacle for all these folks hanging out their windows." But no one watched out the window or watched TV more than Big Ma. Before she got halfway to the car, she told us to keep the Lord with us, night and day. Then she said, "Every good-bye ain't gone."

Fern said, "Surely ain't."

Then Pa drove Big Ma into Manhattan to catch the Greyhound.

MeRRy Like ChRistmas

I, for one, was glad for the Christmas break and that we wouldn't return to school until after the New Year had begun. No one at school could stop talking about the Jackson Five concert, and I was tired of hearing about the songs, the steps, the costumes, and the screaming over Jermaine and Michael. At least they didn't say how dreamy Jackie and Tito were. I would have died on the spot.

Pa and Mrs. tried to make a merry Christmas. Pa had Johnny Mathis singing Christmas carols on our deluxe stereo. Mrs. made the kind of biscuits that pop when you twist the can. Not the kind you set on the windowsill to rise the night before you bake them. That was all right.

Her biscuits still smelled doughy and buttery and would go great with cheese grits and sausage. While I got the grits boiling, Mrs. kept saying, "No, darling. Christmas is for kids doing kid things." But once I had the cheese grated and the sausages dancing in the frying pan, she was anxious for a taste.

Mrs. meant well, but she didn't understand. I had to make the Christmas cheese grits. I wanted something to taste merry like Christmas morning in Big Ma's kitchen.

There was no need to guess which gifts under the tree were from Cecile. Each gift was wrapped in brown paper decorated with either green or red movable type. JOY and VONETTA was printed on the smallest, round gift. MERRY and AFUA was printed on the long, rectangular-shaped gift. PEACE and DELPHINE was printed on the book-shaped gift.

Vonetta pouted because hers was the smallest. That pouting didn't last long when she ripped up JOY and found a gold compact mirror decked in jewels. She fell in love with the jewels and the mirror just like Cecile knew she would.

"Open mine." Fern held out her gift to me.

"You can open it," I said.

"I don't want to tear the part that says 'MERRY.' Like some people I know."

"Baby," Vonetta said, without ungluing herself from

236

her mirror. She had smiled ten different ways before her mirror.

"Open it," Fern told me.

I felt Mrs. looking on. As nice as she was, she would have offered to unwrap the paper for her new "baby," or, as liberated as she was, she would have told Fern to open it herself. I took the brown package and began to pry the tape off the edges. Fern stood over me, breathing hard. Waiting. Once the largest piece of tape was peeled away, Fern snatched the gift from my hand and finished the tape on the ends.

"Tinker Bell!" She held up a case of white pencils from Disneyland with the tiny fairy painted on each pencil.

I was also careful with my wrapping paper. I wanted to keep every green letter whole. I knew Cecile had sent me a book, but I was anxious and hoping I hadn't already read it.

"What did Santa bring you?" Pa asked.

My gift from Cecile was a secondhand copy of *Things Fall Apart*. I raised it up to show him.

"That looks grown," Pa said.

"It's fine literature," Mrs. said.

"Still looks grown."

I read the note from Cecile.

"'I know you'll read this now, but wait two years. Fourteen is a good age to read this book and sixteen is even better. Delphine, you are smart and you are hardheaded. Merry Christmas. Your mother, Cecile.'"

Pa had put together a dollhouse from a kit for Vonetta and Fern to share. The dollhouse was grand, made of metal, and had white aluminum siding on the outside. It had two floors but no staircase. The decorations, the fireplace, rugs, windows, and curtains were all painted on the metal floors and walls. The dollhouse also came with two plastic bags. One bag contained pieces of plastic furniture. The other bag, a tiny pink family ready to move in. Vonetta named them the Taylors, but Fern renamed them the Nixons.

Mrs. threw her hands over her mouth but still managed to laugh out loud. "Get it?" she asked.

"No," Vonetta said. "The Nixons. That don't make no kinda sense."

"In the White House," Fern said.

Even I didn't get it right away, but I eventually caught on.

Then Mrs. said, "Your dad wanted to build a dollhouse."

"I built up *this* house," he said. "I can build a bitty doll-house." That's a pa. Not a dad or daddy.

Vonetta pulled herself away from her mirror and said, "We like this store-bought house better."

"Surely do!"

"Fern," Mrs. said. "What's with this 'surely this' and 'surely that'?"

Vonetta, Fern, and I gave one another a look, then started:

"It's just something she says."

"Like Big Ma says . . ."

"Greedy like a gobbler."

"And untrained chimps."

"It's just a thing Fern says."

"Because it's Fern's thing."

"Surely is."

And without a beat or a signal we went from rat-a-tat-tat to the Isley Brothers' song "It's Your Thing." We even threw in "surely do," in place of the background "doo-hoo-wops."

Mrs. liked the green silk scarf we gave her and modeled it like she was showing off a mink coat on *Let's Make A Deal.* We'd bought the scarf at the church bazaar for thirty-five cents, brought it home, and hand-washed it. I ironed it and then we sprayed it with perfume Big Ma left behind.

We gave Pa a wrench from the church bazaar. He already had wrenches, but that was the only thing he would have found useful. And we had to talk the seller down from a dollar to sixty cents.

Mrs. gave us each a new dress and a poster of the

Jackson Five to hang in our rooms. We screamed as if Jackie, Tito, and their brothers were standing in our living room. Pa said she spent too much money on the dresses and scolded her for bringing those teenage hoodlums inside his house. But I caught him winking at her. Sometimes I didn't know what to make of my father.

Mrs. disappeared into the kitchen and then returned with the telephone receiver, its long, coily cord stretching into the living room. She was smiling like she had a surprise of her own and waved the receiver around. "This is my real gift to you," she said. "Talk as long as you want."

Pa said, "Now hold on a minute, Marva honey."

"It's Christmas, Louis sweetie." She handed the phone to me.

Cecile's was the first voice I wanted to hear. But I couldn't see how Mrs. would know to call the phone booth at Mean Lady Ming's Chinese takeout and tell the first person who answered to run and get Cecile. Nor could I see Cecile standing outside Mean Lady Ming's phone booth at five o'clock in the morning Oakland time to wish us a merry Christmas.

Twelve makes you know better than to wish for things that only eleven would wish hard for.

From the fussing sounds coming out of the receiver, I knew it could only be Big Ma. We could all hear the fussing and we hollered and screamed until Pa said, "All right, girls," in his firm voice. Then we kept it down to hopping like holy rollers, excited to take our turn on the phone.

"Merry Christmas, Big Ma!" we all shouted.

"Merr Christmas," Big Ma said. No merry. Just merr.

"Did you get the gift?" I asked.

Around me my sisters called out:

"Did you like it?"

"I picked it out, Big Ma."

"No. I did."

"I did."

"Delphine, you're hogging up the phone."

"Surely hogging it up."

I had no trouble hearing Big Ma. She spoke loud into the receiver as if the cord wasn't long enough from Autauga County, Alabama, to Brooklyn. I could hear that she was happy and sad, even with my sisters yelping and Johnny Mathis caroling. I could hear her missing us and missing Uncle Darnell.

Real

Mrs. told me to try on her royal blue coat, a winter coat with rabbit fur around the collar and cuffs. I slid my arms into the sleeves. Vonetta and Fern couldn't stop stroking the collar and cuffs. They play-fought over who got to model the coat next, neither of them realizing the gray-and-white fur belonged to a real rabbit. I knew. The fur looked too real, unlike Lucy's pink-dyed jacket that once seemed both dreamy and mod to me. And to Frieda.

"Too grown," Pa said.

"Dear, she's shooting out of her winter coat," Mrs. said.

"She needs a coat for a girl," Pa said.

Pictures flashed in my mind of shopping for school

clothes with Big Ma. Running into Lucy. Lucy picking out my first really nice jumper. Lucy telling me to watch *Hollywood Palace* that night. I missed her. And Frieda. We all made up a long time ago but it was never the same.

"I had it tailored to fit," Mrs. said. "Turn around, darling." Mrs. had a way of not hearing Pa that made me want to smile. It was the way Pa used to have with Big Ma.

"She's a little girl," Pa said.

Vonetta scrunched up her face. "Little?"

"She needs light blue, purple. Pink." Pa was pulling colors out of his head. "Those are nice colors for little girls."

"Popsicle colors!" Fern said. "And sherbet."

My sisters and I laughed at Pa's Popsicle colors, but Mrs. didn't. She said, "I guess it's settled. After we get home from work tomorrow, we'll pick up the girls and run downtown to Macy's, then Gertz to shop. They have a wide array of coats for little girls with all of those Popsicle colors you love. We're bound to find something just right for Delphine. And on sale."

Mrs. had done Pa the way I did Vonetta and Fern. Her words—"wide array," "Macy's," "Gertz," "shop," and "sale"—made Pa stutter.

"N-now, hold on, Marva, honey. L-let's wait a minute. We can't just burn through money." He said that last part without stuttering.

Mrs. gave Pa soft doe eyes that made Vonetta and Fern giggle. "Don't we want *our* girls to be warm for the

243

winter?" she asked, but she wasn't really asking a thing. "Come on, Louis sweetie."

As if we picked up the signal from Mrs., we all sang, *"Pleeease."*

Pa looked both fit to be tied and ready to laugh. I knew he missed having Big Ma on his side of things. He shook his head and said, "My girls. My girls."

In the morning, I stepped into Mrs.'s royal blue coat, now mine, and buttoned its big, round buttons. My arms glided down the sleeves that stopped just over my wrists, like a coat sleeve should. I walked out with my sisters into a whole new year, the rabbit-fur cuffs and collar looking smart and snappy. Once I felt that fur protecting me from the cold, I knew I'd never wear my old coat again. I pulled the fur collar up against my face. I never knew anything could feel so nice.

The sky was a perfect blue, but everywhere else you looked, snow had covered rooftops, parked cars, and driveways. Even the Arabian Knight of Herkimer Street was powdery white. I squinted, blinded by all the snow. The sun had baked a slick ice over patches of sidewalks, so we tried to step on only the snowy, crunchy parts. We were nearing Bedford Avenue when a clump of snow fell from a tree branch and hit the top of Vonetta's cap. I brushed the snow off of it and we crunched snow and slid along until Fern stopped.

"Look!" Fern said. "Uncle D!"

"Where?" Vonetta asked. Three licks of Wanda the Good Switch hadn't done Vonetta any good. I could hear her still wanting to give our uncle a piece of her mind. Or at least punch him one.

Fern pointed her mittened hand toward the redbrick castle. The armory. "There!" Then she pulled down the scarf wrapped around her mouth and hollered, "Uncle D! Uncle Darnell!"

"Is that him?" Vonetta asked.

I cupped my hand over my eyes to fight snow blindness. It only took a second. I put my hand down and shook my head no. The man Fern thought was our uncle was a soldier in a green army uniform. From a distance I could see that he was too big and looked nothing like our uncle.

Vonetta rubbed her gloved fists around and around. "Just wait till I see him. Just wait."

The auditorium roared with kids waiting for the bell to ring. Vonetta and Fern didn't bother with so much as a "See ya, Delphine" once we got inside. They hurried to the front and middle rows where second- and fourth-grade classes sat. I didn't have far to go. The sixth-grade classes sat in the back rows, nearest the exits.

I plunked myself in the aisle seat on the third to the last

row in the middle section. That was where the girls in my class sat. Rukia and Evelyn moved down toward me.

They said their hellos and I said mine.

"Nice coat," Evelyn said, reaching over to pet the cuff.

A skull-capped head turned from the boys' row in front of us. It was Danny the K's head. He said, "Is that your invisible mama's coat?"

I wanted to say, "It's my stepmama's, for your information," but my mouth stopped before it opened. *Stepmama.*

"Why do you wanna know?" Ellis Carter spoke up, then turned to glance at me. "You wanna wear Delphine's pretty blue coat?"

"Oh, snap!" Ant said loudly. "Elly May Clampett snapped on the K."

There was a huge boy ruckus. They pulled off their knitted skullcaps and slapped one another upside the head with them. The boys all laughed and snapped on Ellis and the K, but mostly on the K. Then a PTA volunteer headed up the aisle toward them and the ruckus quieted.

I squirmed in my seat, wondering what had just happened. Did Ellis Carter snap on Danny the K? *For me?*

While the boys, mostly Ellis, took shots at Danny the K, Frieda rose up from her seat next to Lucy and made a motion to her like, "Be right back." She squeezed past all the girls already seated until she stood in the narrow space between me and Rukia and Evelyn. Rukia and Evelyn moved one seat back to let Frieda sit next to me.

246

I thought she was going to start talking but she didn't say anything. Then she ran her fingers around the cuff. "That feels real," she said.

I said, "It is."

On Atlantic Avenue

To Cecile
3 × 1 = 3
3 × 2 = 6
3 × 3 = 9
3 = US
Afua + Vonetta + Delphine
1 = You
Cecile
3 × love
4 U
Happy Valentine's Day!

It was Fern's card, but we all signed our names.

Even though our house is only blocks away from the school, Pa led me around to the front passenger side of the Wildcat, jammed the key in the door lock, and told me to get in. The seat covers were cold when I slid over to unlock the door on the driver's side. I was glad to have my royal blue coat, fur and all.

Vonetta and Fern stood in the doorway, watching. Mrs. appeared and shouted, "Delphine! Wait!" She had something pink and square in her hand. Pa yelled, "We don't have time for that. She'll get it later." Pa's lips tightened. "That woman."

"Get what, Pa?" I asked.

"Some mail I picked up. It'll be there when you get back." He said it like, "Case closed."

I sat back while Pa revved up the Wildcat. On top of butterflies, on top of wanting to go to the dance and not wanting to go alone, I was anxious about what would be waiting for me when I got back.

Papa looked grim, like he was driving me to the state prison, so I didn't press him on what Mrs. had waiting for me. Then I smiled. Big. It was a valentine. Of course it was! I almost didn't care who it came from. A kitchen-printed card from Cecile. A Jesus card from Big Ma. Even a dime-store card from Uncle Darnell, wherever he was. No matter what happened at the dance, I still had a valentine card to come home to.

Vonetta, Fern, and Mrs. huddled in the cold and waved from the door as if I was going to a ball far, far away, but the truth was, they'd still be able to see the Wildcat when we got to the school. The headlights came on and the Wildcat shimmied out of the parking space.

The dark arrived early. It always did that time of year. By six o'clock it seemed like midnight. The insides of our car hadn't warmed up yet but it didn't matter. We'd be there in less than two minutes. I turned the rabbit-fur collar up around my face, against the chill, and wrapped my arms around my waist for the butterflies. We were a block away. I saw kids walking up to the school in pairs and in groups. Some got out of cars. No one walked alone.

Pa and I sat at the stop sign. When it was safe to cruise ahead, Pa put on his blinkers and turned left toward Atlantic Avenue. He pulled the car over but kept the engine running.

He waited for the Atlantic Avenue El train to pass overhead, and told me, "You don't have to go to this school dance."

Mrs. had straightened my hair with Big Ma's hot comb and gave me a flip bang. When I whipped my head to face him the bang was full of bounce and poked me in the eye. I brushed it to the side.

"Papa . . ."

"It's just you and me, Delphine. We can see whatever's playing at the RKO Theatre. Get a bag of popcorn. Some

250

Good & Plenty. Like before." He drummed his fingernails against the steering wheel.

I hadn't had my father to myself in so long. Not to spring out of bed to warm up his dinner when I heard his key in the door. Not to sit in the front passenger side of the Wildcat. For a second, I liked the loneliness of it. The two of us sitting in the cold on Atlantic Avenue. I felt like I'd never have this chance to have him to myself again.

"Just you. Just me," he said. "Up to you, Delphine."

I loved being there with my father, but I chose a long time ago. I was going to the sixth-grade dance, whether anyone asked me to be their special date or not. The worst thing was to not go at all. It would be like everyone else was in the sixth grade and I was in the fifth. That was how Rukia would feel on Monday when everyone else came in still talking about the dance. As sure as I was dressed, my hair looked good, and the dance was going on right around the corner, I knew I wasn't going to the RKO Theatre with my father.

Pa stopped drumming and turned toward me.

I still had my father all to myself. Even if for a few blocks. A few minutes. I knew I could ruin the magic around us, but I had to ask him what Cecile wouldn't tell me. What only he could tell me.

"Why didn't you marry our mother?"

I took him by surprise. He sighed. Shook his head. A sad, slow shake. I couldn't tell if he was angry at me for asking or mad at himself for being caught off guard.

"That's not for you to know," he said.

I had ruined it. My father was trying to rescue me from being a long-legged wallflower and all I had done was make him mad. Or sad.

Still, a stubborn streak showed on my face. He must have seen it and knew I wouldn't stop asking.

"Look at you, Delphine," he said, trying to not be mad at me. "Pretty dress. Hair done up like Diana Ross. . . ."

Tell me, Pa. Please tell me.

I had to know. For me, and for my sisters. "Did you love Cecile, Pa?"

Another sigh.

"I love your mother, Delphine. I do. That's all you need to know," he said.

He glanced at his mirror before pulling the Wildcat out of its spot and making a U-turn. I thought we were going back home. That I had pushed him further than a girl should push her father. Instead, we circled around to get back to the school. I guess Pa just wanted to take the long way.

I saw Evelyn Alvarez and Anthony walking up to the entrance, trailed by Evelyn's three teenage brothers, her chaperones. The Alvarez brothers waited out on the sidewalk until she and Anthony were inside. If Evelyn went with Anthony, then Michael S. must have asked Lucy.

Pa double-parked our car just outside the entrance. I checked the mirror to see if I could get out, but Papa pointed his finger at me and said, "Stay put." He got out of the car, walked around, then opened the passenger door and held out his hand. I couldn't stop smiling. I tried to act like I couldn't see other kids and Evelyn's brothers watching my father taking my arm and escorting me like he was Nat King Cole, but I could feel them all watching.

As we walked toward the door, he said, "Delphine, you need to also know you're a lady. It's always a lady's choice and never the other way around."

I didn't know if he was telling me how to behave at the dance or if he was telling me why he and Cecile never married. I still said, "I know, Papa," just the right way, although I didn't know a thing.

He bent down and gave me a peck on the cheek. "Have a good time, princess." I kissed him back and then I went inside.

Dance, Grade Six

"Delphine Gaither. Six-three."

The PTA mom at the door table smiled up at me, checked off my name, and gave me a red paper heart with my name on it from the shoe box marked 6-3. I unbuttoned my coat and pinned the heart onto the shoulder part of my dress. We'd learned everything we needed to know about the dance at our sixth-grade assembly. If a boy wanted to ask me to dance, he was to walk up to me and first read my name on my heart if he didn't know me. If I was engaged in conversation, he was supposed to say, "Pardon me, Delphine. May I have this dance?" I was supposed to say, "Yes, you may." Last year the boys had to bow and the girls curtsied, but no one would bow or curtsy so they cut that out this year.

All of the hangers on the coatracks along the hallway were already used. I did what others had done and hung my coat over someone else's. If I came with a date, our coats would be hanging together, like Michael S.'s and Lucy's coats probably were.

I entered the gymnasium. Right at the entrance stood a huge heart shape, with *"Happy Valentine's Day, Sixth Graders!"* painted in white, glittery, cursive letters. Ruffled tissue paper had been stapled around the heart, probably by the PTA mom who sat at the table next to it. She had one hand on a big camera strung around her neck, another on top of a collection can.

"Where are your friends, doll?" she asked.

I pointed inside toward the dancing area. "In there, I guess. Dancing."

"Go round them up so I can snap your picture."

"Just me," I said. "I'd like three, please." I wanted my picture taken before my bangs fell and the rest of my hair looked wild from dancing. I took three quarters out of my shoulder purse and dropped them into the PTA can.

"Three?" she hollered. "How many boyfriends you got, doll?"

I smiled big, showing all my teeth. The camera bulb flashed white, blue, and yellow. I blinked at least once, maybe twice while she snapped away. At least I'd have three pictures. One for Cecile. Another for Big Ma. And one to keep.

I'm here, I kept telling myself. *At the sixth-grade dance!* With my eyes temporarily blinded from the flashbulb, I moved toward the center where everyone was. The speakers crackled loud and scratchy while the Archies sang "Sugar, Sugar." All I could see were pink and red hearts hanging from crepe-paper chains, clusters of girls and boys and a few kids dancing in the center, and Principal Myers manning the record player. I closed my eyes, then opened them, searching. I didn't have to search for long. Frieda and Lucy came running toward me. A chaperone said, "Young ladies! No running!"

"Delphine!"

"Your hair!" Lucy bounced my bangs. "You must have Cherokee blood," she said of the straightness, when all I had was Big Ma's hot comb and Mrs.'s curling expertise. Only Lucy would say a thing like "Cherokee blood." She couldn't stop fussing with my hair. "I love it!"

"I like yours too," I said. "Nice dress, Frieda. Yours too, Lucy."

"You know it." Lucy twirled and modeled without shame. "It was the only one like this in the store. I made my mother buy it."

"It could have been the last one," Frieda teased. "Not the only one."

"Well, I'm the only one at the dance wearing it," Lucy said, taking a spin around and pretending to look for anyone wearing her dress. When she stopped spinning, she said, "So, Delphine . . . did you come with anyone?"

There was no sense spinning any straw. Lucy knew no one had asked me to the dance. I shrugged and said, "My father drove me." *Pa* was a word I kept at home.

"You drove here?" Frieda asked. "John-Isaac walked me over."

I offered to give her a ride back but she said her brother would be here looking for her.

"Did Michael bring you?" I asked Lucy.

Frieda's cheeks filled with warm colors. She put her hands over her mouth but laughed anyway. "Tell Delphine what happened!" Frieda said. "Tell her."

Lucy laid the back of her hand against her forehead, flung her head back like an old-time Southern belle, and gasped. "Michael S. comes over and rings the bell," she said. "My mom says, 'Who's that boy ringing my bell?' I say, 'It's my date, Michael S.' My mom says, 'Date? Lucy Ray Raleigh, there's no dating going on under this roof. You're only eleven years old.'"

"All of that while he's waiting on the stoop," Frieda said.

"I'll be twelve in three weeks," Lucy said. "She didn't have to go make a federal case out of it."

"How awful," I said.

"You better believe it," Lucy said. "It was awful. Embarrassing. Mortifying. You know how loud my mother talks."

I said, "Simply mortifying, Lucy Ray Raleigh," in her mother's loud voice. We all laughed. I missed how we used to be with each other. Joking, but underneath it, still friends. I felt like we were back. Really back to being friends.

"So she sent Michael away?" I asked.

Frieda laughed louder than Frieda usually laughs. The same chaperone wagged her finger at us. A fine bunch of young ladies, or as Mr. Mwila would say, "upperclasswomen," we were. "Michael walked her, all right," Frieda said between snorts.

"Yeah. And my mama walked with us."

"In between them!" Frieda said. "So they couldn't hold hands."

Lucy gave Frieda a playful shove. "We weren't going to hold hands."

"You know you wanted to," I teased.

"So what if I did, Miss Too Cute in her Happening Bangs."

The three of us walked around the gym arm in arm, then ran over to the giant valentine and paid a quarter to take a picture together.

To my surprise and horror, Mr. Mwila had come to the sixth-grade dance. The last thing any of us wanted was to see our teacher dance or to know he was watching us dance. When he entered the gymnasium, falling in with the music, bobbing his head slightly, I knew it couldn't be helped. We would have to watch him dance, and I just couldn't picture it. He caught me looking his way and called out, "Save me a dance, Miss Gaither." I nodded and dragged Frieda and Lucy to the refreshments table at the other end of the gym.

We stood over the bowl of candy valentines. I looked into the bowl, searching for the perfect valentine to pick out, but Lucy caught me and said, "No, Delphine. Just close your eyes and pick one." So we each did. Frieda's said "Be Mine." Lucy's said, "Sweet Heart." Mine said, "O U Kid." No one knew what that one meant. We put them on our tongues.

"So your breath will smell like candy when you're dancing the slow dance."

"Slow dance," I said.

We "ewwed" and giggled.

Principal Myers put on a good record. The kind of record that makes a boy want to dance with a girl without feeling stupid. We inched up closer to the circle of dancers waiting, but not too close. Just close enough to join the dancing, and close enough to watch.

Michael S. walked over, I thought, to look for Lucy. But he walked over to Evelyn Alvarez. Instead of asking the way the boys were instructed during the sixth-grade assembly, Michael S. did this head thing. A jerk to the dance floor and Evelyn walked away from Anthony B. and followed Michael S.

Lucy tried to act as though she was looking away, but she was watching them. And then she started chattering about another dress she almost bought and how that color wouldn't go right with her skin tone and the collar was too babyish with all of those bows but her mother really liked that dress. We chatterboxed with her but even though she said yeah in the right places, her eyes were filling up.

Then Anthony B., who had come to the dance with Evelyn and her brothers, headed straight for the punch bowl. We were so busy watching Anthony, no one noticed James T. had walked up to Frieda and asked her to dance, but Frieda said she'd dance the next dance with him. Lucy then pushed Frieda into James T. and they started dancing. All I could think was that was nice of Lucy.

I grabbed Lucy's hand and dragged her out to the center of the dance floor. I sang like Fern, "Lucy, Lucy goosey," in time with the record playing. "Come on. Lucee, Lucee goosey."

She wiped her face quickly and said, "You can't dance with me, Delphine." And she was doing her Lucy-goosey dance. I started to copy her, then she started to laugh, maybe because my arms are so long and I do it a little different. A crowd of girls rushed over, some even leaving their dance partners, and we took turns doing the Lucy goosey, each of us doing it our own way.

Principal Myers put on James Brown's song "There Was a Time," and the girls moved back. Every boy forgot about the girls they wanted to dance with. They peeled themselves off the wall, away from the punch, cookies, and candy, and made it to the center of the dance floor. Whatever dance James Brown called out, the boys from all the sixth-grade classes threw down their Three Musketeers gloves to challenge one another. We watched them dance. The expressions on their faces said "Take that!" "Copy that!" "How ya like that?" as they did the splits, the camel walk, and the mashed potato. All those shoes sliding and scraping up the floor, leaving black shoe polish across the newly varnished floor.

We hollered for all the boys in our class. Anthony, Ant, Enrique, the Jameses, the Michaels, Upton, Willy. All of them. As much as I hated to admit it, Danny the K had the best camel walk of the boys, throwing his head side to side, crunching up his shoulder, sliding across the floor. I forgot how much I couldn't stand him and I cheered along with the six-three girls. Then right in the middle of the K's camel walk, Ellis Carter did a James Brown slide and split out in the center of the floor. Danny knew what was best and camel-walked out of Ellis's way. And when

Ellis rose up, his long legs made a clean triangle, then he snapped his legs together and spun one, two, three times, then did a mashed-potato slide off center stage.

The gym went crazy. We were screaming like Ellis was Jackie Jackson and his brothers rolled up into one. If the PTA were giving out a James Brown trophy, six-three would have won it easily, thanks to Ellis Carter and maybe Danny the K.

After all of that excitement, the principal cooled things down with a slow record—the first slow record of the dance. Boys wiped the sweat and cookie crumbs off their hands and went up to girls to ask them to dance.

Upton walked up to Frieda. "Frieda, may I have this dance?" he asked. She answered, "Yes, you may." Then Michael S. walked over to Lucy and said, "Lucy, may I have this dance?" Lucy rolled her eyes and said, "No, you may not." Then I pushed her into Michael S. and she cut me a glare. But she followed him onto the dance floor.

I watched them all dancing. All dancing in twos. They looked right. The same height for boy-girl dancing. Even the girls dancing in twos looked nice dancing together in their dresses. If Rukia had been allowed to come to the dance and she didn't have a partner, I would have danced with her even though I'm way taller and we would have looked way dumb.

Mr. Mwila walked between the dancers, tapping couples on the shoulder. I could hear him saying, "Decorum," or something like that. Then he looked my way.

I turned away only to face two short boys from class six-five.

"You go ask," one said.

"No. You go."

I felt like a giant. Too tall to look right with anyone. I turned again, wanting to get out of there.

Ellis Carter stood a few feet away from me. He had finished wiping his forehead and his hands with a handkerchief and slipped it into his pocket. He walked up to me.

"Delphine, may I have this dance?" He held out his hand.

I was supposed to say, "Yes, you may," but I sort of nodded and took his hand and we walked out there where everyone danced in twos, each step out to the center in time to the dip of the music, like we were already dancing.

He smiled a little and so did I while we figured out how our hands were supposed to go. Ellis was taller than me. By a full inch. Finally we took one step together. Then another. And another. And another. A perfect box step. And in the middle of the fifth step the slow song faded away. I let go of his hand.

Then Principal Myers put on a fast record. And Mr. Mwila got everyone clapping their hands in rhythm.

Ellis began to clap and so did I.

Then Mr. Mwila called out to all of the PTA moms,

the chaperones, and the other teachers and they all surrounded him.

"This dance," he said, "is from my native Zambia."

Ellis and I looked at each other, mortified. But we still
clapped.

"Here we go," Mr. Mwila said. He shook his hips left,
then right, while doing this marching step that ended in a
hop or a kick. It was hard to tell. Next, the chaperones followed his movements. They were all doing the hop-kick at
the same time. When they were all doing the march-and-
hop, they formed a train, hands on shoulders, and did a
choo-choo or conga around the gym.

"Dance, grade six!" Mr. Mwila shouted. "Dance!"

One by one, the kids caught on and joined the train.
Ellis grabbed my hand and said, "Come on!" Before I
had time to think about it, I placed my hands on Ellis's
shoulders and I marched, kicked, and shook like they did.
Somewhere on the gym floor, doing the dance from Zambia, I lost my red paper heart.

The pink envelope was sitting on my dresser when I got
home. I didn't rush to open it, like I thought I would.
Instead, I arranged my dress on a hanger and hung it on
my doorknob so I could fall asleep looking at it. I took two
sponge rollers and wound my bangs around them.

Then I took the envelope from my dresser, postmarked
Oakland, CA. The handwriting was cursive and extra neat.

Neither the address nor the handwriting were Cecile's. I pried the pink envelope open carefully, not wanting to tear a thing, and pulled out the card. I didn't expect anything, but if I had, I would have expected he'd send me a funny valentine. But I wouldn't call his valentine card funny. Not at all.

Who's Loving You?

Dear Delphine,

I would have picked a different dress for you. A differ-
ent color. A different style. And your hair is too grown
for your face. You're just a minute past twelve taking
on Sweet Sixteen. Sixteen wasn't sweet on me, but I
want yours to be nothing but sweetness, in time.
Time turns always, Delphine. Don't push it.
The palm tree in my yard keeps trying to stand up in
spite of a cold couple of months. We'll see how it's lean-
ing in the spring.
Look after Vonetta. Fern can look after herself.
Study your lessons.

Your Mother,
Cecile.

P.S. The Woods boy said hello.

I was in the kitchen making our after-school snack when the doorbell rang. I hurried into the parlor and pulled back the curtain. A white special-delivery jeep stood double-parked outside. I went to the front door, unbolted the top and bottom locks, and turned the knob. The door chain only allowed a few inches between the postman and me.

"Special delivery," the postman said. "Sign here."

Our neighborhood postman was probably used to being met with chains over cracked doors. He slid the clipboard and pen through the space. "Print, then sign," he said.

I printed and signed my name and passed the clipboard and pen back to him. "You can leave it," I said, and closed the door. Once he was back inside his jeep, I unlatched the chain, opened the door, and picked up the package. It was a white box. The kind they sell at the post office. It was square, like a kitchen floor tile, but bigger and two inches deep, like a cereal box. The right-hand corner of the box was decorated with a mess of stamps. Probably more than it needed. The words WALTER REED

HOSPITAL and a Washington, DC, postmark in broken letters showed through faintly over the stamps. There was no return address or sender's name in the upper left-hand corner, the way a package or letter should be addressed. Just *To Miss Vonetta Gaither* with our address on Herkimer Street, Brooklyn, NY, in black ink, dead-center of the package. The handwriting wasn't a hundred percent straight, but it wasn't wavy.

"VONETTA!"

I shouted louder than I should. Big Ma would have cocked her head and said, "This isn't no jungle and you're not Tarzan," or something like that. But Big Ma's chair stayed empty. I only heard her in my head and once a month on the telephone.

Vonetta beat Fern out into the living room. I handed her the white box. "It's for you, Net-Net," I said.

"Don't call me that," she snapped.

I felt sorry for her. I was mad at our uncle but now I was more sad about him than mad at him. The way Pa was over Cecile, probably. I didn't like Uncle Darnell for what he did, but I knew I still loved him. I knew I wanted him to be my uncle. The way he once was.

Vonetta took the box and shook it. She looked at her name. I wondered if she knew who'd sent it. I wondered if she'd want what was inside if she knew.

"Open it!" Fern cried, dancing on her feet like one of Tina Turner's Ikettes. "Open it up now!"

"I will," Vonetta said. She was trying to be cool, but she was as curious as we were. The tape that ran across the flaps and sides was the sturdy, good tape with string glued into it. Vonetta tried to scratch a piece of the tape, but she couldn't catch hold of it. Fern and I hovered over her, waiting.

"I'll help you," I said.

"No," she said, hugging the box away from me. "You're not the only one who can do things, Delphine."

I would have popped her upside the head but Cecile had said to keep an eye on her. I just gave Vonetta a look. She gave me one back. Cecile was wrong. It was Vonetta and not I who was hardheaded.

"Open it!" Fern shouted still dancing.

"I will if you two stop breathing on me."

Vonetta picked at the tape and shook the box again, as if that would help. I went and got the long, metal nail file and handed it to her, hoping she wouldn't poke herself with it. I'd be on punishment for days if Pa and Mrs. came home and found Vonetta's hand bandaged up.

Determined to prove she didn't need my help, Vonetta stubbornly grunted and stabbed away at the taped flaps. Finally, one of the flaps had had enough and caved in after all of that poking and stabbing. Vonetta pulled out what was inside the square package.

We all screamed. And jumped, and screamed some more.

Jackie Jackson and his brothers. There was Jackie Jackson. And Tito.

We screamed for the longest time. Jackie. Jermaine. Tito. Marlon. Michael. Right here in our living room. If this wasn't a grand Negro spectacle, I didn't know what was. As long as Big Ma wasn't here to see it or stop it, we continued to jump, scream, and holler.

After we made ourselves hoarse, Fern said, "Put it on."

I reached for the album cover but Vonetta snatched it up. "I'll do it," she said.

Between us, I was the only one allowed to turn on the deluxe stereo. If Vonetta broke the needle we'd never be allowed to play the stereo again and I'd probably catch Lightning for sure. But I had to let Vonetta put the record on this time. "So do it," I said.

She opened the stereo case. The same stereo case that filled the house with blue smoke when Cecile played Sarah Vaughn and Nina Simone while she tapped out her rhythms and wrote poems on Cream of Wheat boxes and on the walls. The same stereo that Uncle Darnell played the Coasters and the Orlons on even when those records went out of style. The same stereo Big Ma called "the devil's worldly jukebox" but asked Uncle D to put Mahalia Jackson and Shirley Caesar on. Pa'd take the stereo apart to replace pieces and clean the insides, but he hardly ever spun any records on the turntable. Only Johnny Mathis on Christmas.

I held my breath while Vonetta slid the shiny black LP

270

out of its paper sleeve and placed it onto the turntable.

The record began to spin. Vonetta picked up the cover, ran her finger along the list of songs. When she reached for the turntable's arm, I couldn't help myself and said, "Don't scratch it."

She gave me that teeth-sucking sound, and Fern said, "Ooh," probably expecting me to pop her one. I didn't.

Vonetta remained cool and then blew dust off the needle to show me she knew what she was doing. She counted along the spinning record. Counted the right number of strips on the disc that separated one song from the next. When she found the song she wanted to play first, she gently placed the needle down. I knew she'd never be this careful with the needle again.

Then the piano keys trilled and the guitar and bass and drums pounced on the downbeat and I forgot all about Vonetta, the record needle, and getting in trouble. We all did. The Jackson Five was in our living room on Herkimer Street.

We must have worn the record out playing each song over and over. It was near time for Pa and Mrs. to walk in, so we chose the last song.

"Who's Loving You" is the perfect Vonetta song. It begins with Michael letting go of all the air in his lungs to lay open his soul and sing one word: "When." Kind of like Vonetta howling in her crib to be picked up or howling for a cookie.

Vonetta and Fern traded off between the high Michael parts while I sang the lower background parts. As young as they were, it was funny to listen to Vonetta, Fern, and Michael sing about how they've been lonely all their lives. I felt like I was watching my sisters singing, really singing, and not clowning. That somehow it would be ruined if they caught me watching them. I didn't want Vonetta or Fern to stop singing, so I closed my eyes.

I sang and thought, What did little Michael Jackson know about love and loneliness? With all his brothers surrounding his voice with theirs, what did he know about losing all the people he loved one by one?

We sang the highs and the lows with Michael, whose voice was big and filled with pain like he might know what he was singing about. Even so, I couldn't stop asking myself, What did Michael Jackson know about life without the ones you loved the most, when each of them moved farther and farther away until they were voices you heard and pictures that flashed before you? Vonetta knew. Fern knew. I knew. There wasn't a day that went by that we didn't wonder about everyone who had flashed before us. There wasn't a day that went by that we didn't close our eyes and go wishing.

Author's Note

When my editor, Rosemary Brosnan, emailed me illustrator Frank Morrison's preliminary jacket sketch of Delphine, Vonetta, and Fern jumping double Dutch in bell-bottoms on Herkimer Street, I said immediately, "This is it!" It didn't matter that Big Ma would have never let her grands wear bell-bottoms; Frank Morrison captured both the spirit of the Gaither sisters in Bedford-Stuyvesant and the spirit of the late 1960s and early 70s, which so complements my approach to this story. Although *P.S. Be Eleven* resumes where *One Crazy Summer* ends, this sequel yearns to reflect the spirit of that period. I've exercised literary license to bring together events and details that reflect the happenings within the Gaither home, the Bedford-Stuyvesant community, and the nation. As Oakland represented the Black Panthers and the Black Power movement in *One Crazy Summer*, Bedford-Stuyvesant during these volatile years embodies the riots, racial strife between African-Americans and Jews, and the urban blight in this community. On his many trips to Brooklyn, Senator Robert F. Kennedy met with local leaders in Bedford-Stuyvesant to bring economic, education, and housing solutions to the then-depressed area. Today, a sculpture of Senator Kennedy stands in Restoration Plaza on a thriving Fulton Street—one block away from Herkimer Street.

Acknowledgments

Although the story and characters in *P.S. Be Eleven* come from my imagination, I am beholden to various individuals I've met on Herkimer Street, specifically Julie on Troy Avenue and Mark on New York Avenue, for sharing their recollections of Bedford-Stuyvesant of the past. Both Brooklynites generously gave me their time and answered my many questions, but both declined to give their last names. I am especially grateful for the extensive resources of the Brooklyn Collection at the Brooklyn Public Library at Grand Army Plaza, and for its amazing research librarian, June Koffi, who scoured the "morgue" for precious articles to aid me in my storytelling. I must thank Peter Garcia, for answering my military-related questions as well as for talking about his days of summer employment in Brooklyn as a teen during the early seventies. I also posthumously thank my mother, Miss Essie, for not throwing out my diaries and trunkful of writing. Those writings allowed me to tap into ages eleven and twelve in 1968 and 1969.

I thank my fellow writers at the Vermont College of Fine Arts for creating a community around me of people who think in story.

Most of all, I am boundlessly appreciative of everyone at HarperCollins for supporting *P.S. Be Eleven* wholeheartedly and believing there was more to tell about Delphine, Vonetta, and Fern. I am especially indebted to Susan Katz, Kate Jackson, Barbara Lalicki, Patty Rosati, Molly Thomas, Robin Pinto, Stephanie Macy, Tony Hirt, Kim VandeWater, Andrea Martin, and soul sister number one, Rosemary Brosnan, who also shares these memories.

Go back to where it all began with the Gaither sisters

Awards and Honors for

ONe CRazy SummeR

Newbery Honor Book

Coretta Scott King Award (Author)

National Book Award Finalist

Scott O'Dell Award for Historical Fiction

Named a Best Book of the Year by: *Boston Globe, Christian Science Monitor, The Horn Book, Kirkus Reviews, Publishers Weekly, School Library Journal,* and *Washington Post*

ALA Notable Book

Chicago Public Library Best of the Best

New York Public Library's "One Hundred Titles for Reading and Sharing"

New York Times **Editors' Choice**

NAACP Image Award Nominee

Parents' Choice Gold Award

"A powerful and affecting story of sisterhood and motherhood."
—Monica Edinger, *New York Times*